"The tree of liberty must be refreshed from time to time with the blood of patriots and tyrants"

Thomas Jefferson

Texas:
A Free Nation Under God

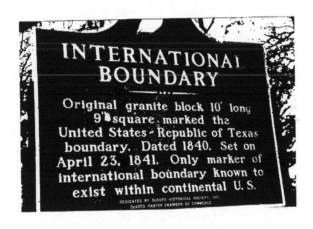

Manuel L. English, PhD
With
Chris Adams, Major General, USAF (Ret)

authorHOUSE®

AuthorHouse™
1663 Liberty Drive
Bloomington, IN 47403
www.authorhouse.com
Phone: 1-800-839-8640

First published by AuthorHouse 8/05/2011

ISBN: 978-1-4634-1173-2 (sc)
ISBN: 978-1-4634-1172-5 (hc)
ISBN: 978-1-4634-1171-8 (e)

Library of Congress Control Number: 2011907939

Printed in the United States of America

Dedication

We dedicate this book to those Texans who were there at the beginning when Texas won its freedom from Mexico. These noble souls include our own distant relatives who fought and died at the Alamo, were massacred at Goliad, and were at the side of General Sam Houston when he captured General Santa Ana at San Jacinto. We also pay special tribute to the many Texans who have served our country in the uniforms of our military services in war and in peacetime. Those who work hard to maintain our traditional values and our system of beliefs are also recognized and appreciated. Texas will always hold a special place in the hearts of the authors because it is where they shed their youthful tears and grew up to appreciate a sense of responsibility and pride in their distinguished Texas heritage. We also hope that Texas will always retain its special place in an ever changing world.

Table of Contents

Dedication v
Prologue...ix
Chapter One 3
Chapter Two 11
Chapter Three 19
Chapter Four...27
Chapter Five...37
Chapter Six 51
Chapter Seven 55
Chapter Eight..65
Chapter Nine 75
Chapter Ten 85
Chapter Eleven..93
Chapter Twelve 103
Chapter Thirteen.. 109
Chapter Fourteen 129
Chapter Fifteen 141
Epilogue.. 149
Texas History Timeline.. 153
List of Texas Revolution battles 169
About the Authors.. 173

Prologue

In the last general election Texans voted overwhelmingly for the republican war hero candidate to replace their fellow Texan president who was ending his two terms in office. It became clear in early returns from just a handful of states that their candidate would not win.

This particular general election campaign had raised many contentious issues espoused by the newly elected democrat president and along with a democrat congress they collectively went about making major changes in national social and economic policies. For many Texans these changes were akin to socialism itself. Several new government programs created even more debt as well as outright loss of personal freedom and the basic rights to believe in and practice long-held traditions. Of even greater concern was the diminishing of national security which was troubling to even the most open-minded conservative Texans and lawmakers.

The changes being imposed by the new administration included, amongst other things, the creation of a nationalized health care system and a withdrawal of U.S. military forces from Afghanistan. Sensitive and troubling issues also included canceling the "don't ask; don't tell" policy within the military services, federal funding of abortion, recognition of gay marriage, free pass for illegal immigrants already living in the United States, closing of the Guantanamo terrorist detention center and trying terrorists in the U.S. courts. Many Texans and southerners were also alarmed over the appointment of two liberal supreme court judges believing that their traditions would be further eroded. It was clear to most that the overall objective was to centralize more federal and presidential executive power in Washington, D.C., thereby leaving states like Texas without any say in these and other liberal changes.

The unstable environment and a disorganized republican party left the political door wide open for the democrat congress to mount an aggressive legislative agenda to support their like-minded president.

With each legislative session, political conservatives in Texas became more concerned with and paid closer attention to the far-reaching economic, social and domestic programs being enacted by the democrats and their president. During the first two years of the president's term, Texans watched and waited for some counter-balancing power to begin challenging these new liberal legislative actions. However, there were no overt actions to cause a slowdown much less halt the rapid-paced changes. The minority republican party in both the house and the senate seemed at best ineffectual.

These issues were openly and privately discussed when Texas Governor Patrick Shahan called his first post election special legislative session. The majority of Texas lawmakers focused on specific issues and the much broader implications of a complete liberal takeover of the country. A small number of senators and representatives from the largely liberal enclaves of Austin and Houston were somewhat reluctant to criticize programs that they mostly agreed with. Of major concern for the conservatives was the impact of such programs on Texas culture and traditions. Inaction, finger-pointing, and confusion followed the special meeting with no particular initiatives or changes put forth. Meanwhile, the administration in Washington continued on their uninhibited march daringly strutting their stuff.

During a second special session which followed a year later, many Texas legislators had learned well that their constituents were becoming increasingly agitated and could no longer accept the onerous changes coming from Washington. Frustration generated fresh political philosophies to challenge the lackadaisical approach they felt conservative legislators were taking instead of fighting back. There was much beneath-the-surface political activity taking place within Texas with very little concern regarding where it was heading and where it might end.

A few months later, national mid-term elections were held and found republicans taking back control of the House of Representatives. This gave a brief sigh of relief to many conservatives as they began to see hope that just perhaps this president may not be elected for second term.

However, in many parts of the country the euphoria over the democratic president remained undaunted. During his first two years he had a commanding majority in the House and Senate which gave him the support to continue bringing about his vision of change. Now it would be a bit more difficult, but still doable his supporters believed. Governor Shahan did not have much hope that the new republican congress would gain the momentum or possess the courage to effectively challenge the president's programs. The president's ill-conceived policies continued to weigh heavily on conservatives across the country; especially in Texas. The nation's downward spiraling economy continued to cause world-wide havoc. The president's recent actions since the mid-term election had produced a small upward gain on Wall Street; yet, many were still impatiently waiting for the economy, especially the labor market and hiring to rebound.

Home prices had now depreciated nearly 40 percent in many areas of the country—California, Nevada, the upper Midwest and East Coast, being hit the hardest. The administration continued to initiate horrific borrowing from the Federal Treasury into the trillions of dollars to "stimulate" the flagging economy believing that these bold initiatives would be in effect an "investment by the American people" to bring the economy back in line. In many cases, these so-called investments only caused more national debt which is now 15 trillion dollars.

The ongoing war against terrorism now principally focused on Afghanistan and liberals were pushing for a date to withdraw our troops. Many conservatives growing weary of the ten-year-plus war that was costing lives and money were cautiously pleased and surprised by the president's initiative to begin using un-manned drones to kill insurgents. In May 2011, the news that Osama bin Laden had been killed provided some political momentum for the president, however, others speculated that the administration knew for some time where bin Laden was located, but waited to take this action until it was closer to the next election believing the news would help bring about a second term for this president. This point was somewhat proven in the days following the announcement in that the administration milked every aspect of it to fit within their political agenda. The political theme they seemingly wanted to get out to the voting public was the president was solely responsible for the demise of bin Laden. Others believed this was a strategy that would allow the president to claim warrior status and thus help legitimize his eventual decision to bring the troops home, most probably after the next general election when the political stakes are lower. Offsetting these considerations was the continued concern over the president's tepid response to the political and social changes erupting in the Middle East which added fuel to those who held doubts about his leadership.

On the broader world front, old enemies and resurging new ones alike closely observed the behavior of the U.S. president with opportunistic eyes. The Russians after two decades following their cold war collapse and the loss of prestige and their grip on Eastern Europe continued to harbor grudges against the United States. Iran and North Korea likewise had 'teased' the U.S. throughout the previous republican president's two terms. With this president, they did not hesitate to flex their muscles and try to 'cash in' on the situation they believed was ripe for exploitation.

The administration continued to be plagued by not only their own missteps but by outside influences which caused embarrassment. Notably was the shocking release of secret and confidential information via "WikiLeaks," the devious project by an Australian internet guru who, through nefarious means, had for months 'tapped' into high level government e-mail channels and data banks and now for fame and a price he was peddling his findings. This 'alleged' international non-profit organization began publishing sensitive and classified information pertaining to communiqués to, from, and between U.S. allies and enemies alike. With each new revelation of private, secret, and classified documents from anonymous sources, it was clear that more 'information' would be released in the upcoming months.

The historic burdening economic issues, potential threats from the outside along with the president forging ahead with a multitude of social and domestic legislation and implementing governmental health care while ignoring an out-of-control migration of *illegals* continued to highlight the nationwide issues facing the president. Texas had fared reasonably well through the economic down-turn; job losses were at a minimum across the spectrum of businesses and the petroleum industries continued to prosper with ever-increasing discovery and drilling for natural gas. Agricultural crop production remained good and product manufacturing also continued at a moderate rate. While patriotic Texans still supported the committed war on terror efforts, it was the dramatic changes in social values being promulgated by the president's staff and appointees and their impact on Texans that worried them most. How many more of these radical changes are we willing to take was the subtle question being heard more and more across Texas, especially in small towns and rural areas. Many openly suggested drastic changes were necessary to stop the federal government from taking away their traditional beliefs and way of life. Few speculated as to just what form these changes would and should take.

Chapter One

BAM! The oversized oak gavel in the right hand of the Speaker of the House slammed down on its sturdy base, echoing throughout the vast chamber; momentarily interrupting the loud chatter.

"The special call session of the State Legislature of Texas is closed. The..." Speaker Manuel Estrada attempted to continue, but was drowned out by howling outbursts of yelps and shouts.

"Hear! Hear!" The Speaker shouted; his piercing eyes and visible furrows on his sweaty forehead revealing frustration. "Hear! Hear!" Banging down the huge gavel several more times, the chorus of babble with only a few rude outbursts finally quieted down as the harried Speaker attempted to continue the closing formalities.

"The Regular Session of this body will convene on January 19th. God bless Texas!" Estrada snapped his final remarks in an agitated voice, pounding down the gavel for the last time. Once again the gallery erupted in noisy chatter along with a few shouts.

The special session had been turbulent; even more so than a few years back when democrat legislators revolted against the republican lead legislative redistricting initiative and set up a caucus across the border in Oklahoma. The anger coming from the conservative majority was not so much on what was happening in Texas politics, but in the country as a whole which they seemingly couldn't do anything about. Manuel Estrada, a serious-minded, handsome young lawyer turned politician had sought the speaker position of leadership, perhaps to prove his worth as a minority as much as anything else. He recently confided to close confidants that this had been the worst year of his life.

Hispanic and a conservative to the core, Estrada had tried in vain to be the *good guy,* as any house leader should be—listening patiently to all sides and to mediate—become the ultimate arbiter in fairness. The democrat legislators were only a few short of equaling the republican majority and were overwhelmingly vocal against virtually any program voiced by the republican governor and the house majority; especially the purpose for convening a special session to address the drug wars taking place on the Texas/Mexico border and immigration reform. Some democrat legislators in the Texas House agreed with the do-nothing approach the federal government was now taking. They also had the ear of the always seeking, searching for controversy, Austin and the state-wide pockets of a *laissez-faire* media who publically supported the democrat agenda. The view of the liberal minority in the Texas legislature like their liberal friends in Washington was to forgive the mass of *illegals* that persistently migrate across the Rio Grande by the thousands and to work out an immunity plan to let them remain. There was also a critical problem developing along the Mexico-Texas border involving drug dealers, cartels and trafficking with hundreds of law enforcement officers and numerous other innocent people being killed on both sides of the border. Even this issue was not enough to divert them from illusionary thinking.

"After all," the liberal lawmakers argued echoing what was coming out of Washington; "they provide us with an unlimited source of cheap labor and we do not want to upset or show prejudice toward any group of citizens."

"True," came back strong-minded conservatives, "but they are also taking away jobs from our own people, impact our school systems and they are straining our medical services to a breaking point. They pay no taxes and the crime rate in South Texas is rampant and growing state-wide; if the feds don't take immediate action, then we are going to be forced to! At least the governor is cognizant; even in his time of illness, he is listening to reason. We must act now to change direction or Texas will be overrun by illegal immigrants and Mexican drug cartels; both are impacting the state's economy and threatening the general well-being of Texans across the state. Juarez, just across the border from El Paso, had become a *killing field* in its own right besides the growing unrest along the Mexican side of the Rio Grande."

House republican committees were reviewing and considering adopting an employment verification system called 'e-verify' to help keep illegals out of the workplace. But this piece of legislation was unlikely to pass both houses.

The illegal issue made the task of Speaker Estrada even more difficult; after all, he was Hispanic and the liberals couldn't understand why he was not one of them. He was the son of Mexican immigrants and was raised on a cattle ranch in the Big Bend where his father worked as a cowhand and his mother as a maid for the ranch owner family.

"Manny" as he was called, became the favorite of rancher Craig Cabot, a tall suntanned cowboy and an arch conservative delighted in instilling strong, independent values in his bright young protégé. Manny was a hard worker which helped him to excel in school and athletics, and he was offered a scholarship to the University of Texas to play football; however his mentor, Cabot, urged him to attend Sul Ross State College at nearby Alpine and "stay away from those 'liberals over in Austin," he told Estrada.

"I'll take care of all his expenses," Cabot told Manny's parents. "I want that boy to grow smart with Texas values and earned responsibilities," he said.

Manny respected Cabot and was content to attend Sul Ross; he worked on the ranch in the summers, excelled in football and academics, graduating with honors. "Now that you have grown up and know better," Cabot grinned, "you need to go on over to Austin and knock hell out of 'em in that liberal-minded UT law school—make your folks and me proud. Just don't forget your roots."

Manny Estrada did just that; married his college sweetheart, Maria, and joined a law firm back in Alpine. After a few years of practicing law, Craig Cabot convinced him to run for the legislature, which he did and won handily. He sought the house speaker position after a few years and was elected by his peers.

The rant continued between the two sides throughout the four-week June special session with little satisfaction, much less action by the lawmakers. In the end, Speaker Estrada concluded the session as the national political campaign season moved into full swing with several candidates promising to make the immigration issue a first priority in the forthcoming state legislative session.

Over on the senate side where conservatives held an overwhelming majority, the environment had been somewhat quieter and demure, but the underlying contentious issues were ingrained in the thoughts of each senator. Governor Shahan was extremely ill and had called another special session of the senate and house to share his parting views and concerns for his beloved Texas. Lt. Governor Bill Simmons, presiding, was a close friend of the governor; they had been fellow state senators and Simmons conducted the state's business according to their mutual desires.

Governor Patrick Shahan was in his second term and had been diagnosed with lung cancer a year before. As time passed following the completion of the first legislative session, his illness took a turn for the worse and he knew that he had only a few months, if that. Shahan was born in East Texas and knew that the people of his state, particularly those serving in both houses of the legislature, were growing more and more concerned if not outright angry with the ongoing changes coming from the liberal majority in Washington, which were thought of as an anathema to the people of Texas. In the privacy of his thoughts and in his discussions with the lieutenant governor, he sought ways to keep his people free from such tradition-changing legislation and prevent its impact on the time-honored social and family values which were embedded in the Texas way of life. Yes, he was concerned about the border situation and the problem with drug cartels and illegals, but it was the happenings in Washington that were literally causing conservative Texans to shake their head in bewilderment. 'Change' was upon them and they were scared of what was to come next.

Governor Shahan was fully cognizant of the growing unrest among his fellow Texas republicans and the potential drastic actions that several prominent members of his own party were openly postulating. Lt. Governor Simmons kept him fully briefed on the discussions taking place in and out of the Austin. Shahan called this special legislative session on the pretext of addressing immigration issues, but now his main concern was to calm their emotions.

Governor Shahan had managed the strength to open the special session with words of encouragement and optimism. "As you know, my fellow legislators, I am not well," he told the joint session of the two legislative branches, "but I have the strength of my convictions that our great nation and Texas will not only endure this turbulent period of time where fear and confusion are paramount, but at some point in the future we will prevail. As individuals and as partisan representatives of our people we cannot and should not agree with much of the rhetoric being generated in Washington..." He was abruptly interrupted by outbursts of *Nay's* from several in the gallery.

"Please gentlemen, and ladies, let's be civil. I have called this special session to principally address the growing impositions from Washington impacting our state and to hopefully unify our people throughout Texas to rally against this onslaught of liberal changes. Lt. Governor Simmons and I are both greatly troubled with almost every legislative act coming out of Washington. I know that many of you share this concern. I challenge each of you sitting before me to work toward solutions that meet the needs and expectations of all Texans. We must not forget that it is to the people of Texas where we must look to find our will and strength and our values. However, while we may not always agree with the direction Washington wishes to take us, we must strive to work within the system and ourselves to achieve the best for all. Regardless of the outcome of past national elections and our own elections within the state, we must work to seek unity. I thank each of you for coming back to your capital for this abbreviated session and I impose on your respective leaders to guide you through the legislative processes with success being a noble goal. Now go to work and serve your state. Thank you, goodbye and God bless Texas!"

His closing words carried the despair of finality as he bowed slightly to the assembly of lawmakers, eased back from the lectern unsteadily and departed smiling as he politely elbowed away any attempt to assist him. The gallery responded with a standing ovation.

The session did not go as the governor had hoped; rather it mainly provided an opportunity for lawmakers to be in Austin and to gather in after-hour splinter groups to address the much broader ill-conceived social changes brought on by the liberal president; especially his overriding agenda of "change" that bore against the grain of independent, self-reliant Texans; even some liberals quietly expressed equal concerns with the actions being taken by the president.

Among the numerous state leaders opposing the growing imposition of liberal values and social legislation is Attorney General of Texas,

Della Murphy, a 7th generation Texan. She was openly outspoken with a persuasive, tenacious manner voicing abhorrence toward the issues that were now becoming law by the democrat president and forced on the nation and people of Texas.

She stood firm with her convictions. "The winds of liberal change are blowing through Texas which if not stopped, will forever change its people and our culture," stated the plainspoken lady when addressing a State Republican Women's Forum. "We cannot let this happen to our state and to the people we represent. We must explore alternatives to this democrat driven social onslaught to insure the preservation of our Texas traditions and history."

Her remarks were repeated on the local Austin TV news caught national attention and Texas legislators on both sides of the aisle because she was one of the emerging voices in State government. With an exceptionally bright legal mind, Attorney General Murphy was a former district attorney in Houston. She grew up in South Texas, the daughter of sharecropper parents, with a half dozen brothers and sisters. She moved from rural poverty, became a high school beauty queen and valedictorian; onward to earn her juris doctorate from the University of Texas. In her mid-forties, married to an attorney and the mother of two, she is attractive, and much at ease in expressing herself clearly in a Texas drawl. A female and republican, she won her election to become state attorney general overwhelmingly. From her compelling and directly stated positions most knew that Della Murphy would be a growing major force in Texas politics.

On the very evening the special session finally closed, Governor Shahan died. The event, although expected in the near term, still caught lawmakers and the state at large by surprise. Hastily, arrangements were made to swear in Lt. Governor Bill Simmons late that same night. The following day, Simmons declared a 30-day state of mourning to honor his friend and the former governor. Many of the lawmakers were still in Austin and remained until final funeral arrangements were completed.

Bill Simmons was a popular, well-liked and respected politician who was prepared to assume the governorship without any hesitation.

He grew up in Panola County, Texas, played high school football and graduated from Baylor University. He enlisted in the Marine Corps at the onset of the Vietnam conflict and served four years including eighteen months in combat, earning the Silver Star. Returning home, he met and married a local school teacher, entered Baylor Law School and practiced criminal law for a time before campaigning for election as State Representative from his home district. Following three terms as a representative, he successfully ran for state senator and afterward, lieutenant governor. At sixty-seven he still looked fit and trim.

When word reached Lieutenant General Chris Mitchell, a native Texan and close friend of Governor Shahan, he promptly headed for Austin from Washington to be with the governor's family. General Mitchell had become acquainted with the governor, then a state senator, while he was stationed at several different Air Force bases in the state over the years. Their interaction developed into a trusted friendship. Mitchell grew up in a small Southeast Texas town, attended a state teachers college and received a commission in the U.S. Air Force following graduation. He attended pilot training and spent the majority of his career as a bomber pilot in Strategic Air Command before moving on to several command and staff positions. He was now in Washington DC and assigned to the Joint Chiefs of Staff as Director of Plans.

The Director of the Texas National Guard, Major General Tom Lawhorn, who was based at Camp Mabry near Austin, was quick to say that he would attend the funeral services. Lawhorn, a weather-beaten, hard-charging natural leader who looked older than his years, was a native of McAllen where his father was employed as an agent of the U.S. Agriculture Department. His mother was a naturalized Hispanic. Working hard was part of his grain which helped him excel in high school and earn an appointment to the United States Military Academy at West Point. Upon graduation, he served in a number of assignments in the infantry and armored cavalry before requesting transfer to the Army National Guard. Moving up through the ranks with increasing responsibility, he was eventually appointed by Governor Shahan as the Adjutant General of Texas. Immediately after Governor Simmons was sworn in he called General Lawhorn asking him to continue serving in his position. Lawhorn readily agreed to do so.

During the few hours preceding the burial service for Governor

Shahan, the newly inaugurated Governor Simmons, Attorney General Murphy, Generals Mitchell and Lawhorn engaged in separate and collective casual conversations that had begun to occupy most everyone's thoughts in recent months including where the country is headed under the democratic president and democratic congress. These brief encounters brought together both old and new friends, and set the stage for evolving into more serious talks.

Governor Shahan was laid to rest with full state and military honors, reflecting the great respect and affection that his colleagues, friends, and the people of Texas held for him.

Chapter Two

Although Governor Simmons had given some thought to potential candidates whom he might consider for nomination to replace himself as lieutenant governor, he wasn't ready to move that quickly until Attorney General Murphy reminded him on the morning of Governor Shahan's funeral..."Sir, you should name a candidate fairly quickly for continuity," she said.

"I will, Della," he replied, somewhat annoyed by her insistence. "Let's talk after the service. But first, I would like to gather a few special people for a brief meeting while they are here in town, including you, of course, to discuss some of the issues that Pat Shahan, you, I, and many others, have had in common thought over the past several months. I have asked Gene Todd to set up a meeting in my office this evening. After that, I will get to the nomination process. Let's follow up in the morning."

With bold confidence, Governor Simmons on impulse invited the small 'coalition of friends' including his public affairs officer, Gene Todd, to meet with him in the capitol building that evening following the service. He had observed Della, General Mitchell, and General Lawhorn closely interacting since they arrived for the funeral.

At first the tempo of the gathering was awkward as the group assembled in Governor Simmons' small private side office. No one knew exactly what the impromptu meeting was all about. Already comfortable with each other, the small group relaxed with wine and small talk; the conversation centering mostly on the loss of Governor Shahan. No one questioned the perceived *real* purpose for the gathering, though each instinctively felt they had been invited for something other than a formal reception. Spouses had been excluded when the verbal invitations were carefully and quietly extended to each one individually.

The cordial formalities took on a serious quality when Attorney General Murphy suddenly spoke, "Governor, just a word of caution, if this gathering should become public for any reason—whatever its intended purpose—a private closed meeting between state officials and U.S. military officers; it could result in a negative interpretation. You know the media hounds."

"I agree Della, thank you," Simmons replied, nodding. "You are absolutely correct and that is why I have asked Gene Todd to join us in the event some of the media should decide to make their own interpretations of our *social* gathering. I hope, if this meeting should attract some attention, or anyone of us is questioned, we will simply respond that we gathered as close friends to lament the death of our cherished colleague, Pat Shahan; right Gene?"

"Right, Governor," Todd responded. "I'll have a cover story prepared just in that event; so if any of you should get pestered, please let me know."

"By the way," Simmons quickly followed. "I should have formally introduced Gene Todd to you when we first arrived, but I see that he has already made himself known to you personally. Gene is the guy we rely on to get the word out and to correct those in the media that don't get it quite right. Thank you, Gene."

"Governor, forgive me; for the benefit of the others here who don't know me that well," Attorney General Murphy smiled as she again spoke. "I tend to frequently cut to the chase and impatiently so. I welcome the opportunity to visit with you and hopefully to not preempt the governor's remarks with regard to this gathering. The governor is well aware of my feelings and concerns about the liberal movement in our country and its grave impact on Texas. I hope this meeting is directly or somewhat related to this." "It is." replied the governor. "Good," Della continued. "I have been quite vocal, perhaps too much so, regarding my thoughts and concerns. I am doubly pleased and impressed with the presence of our fellow Texans from Washington and elsewhere and permit me to ask, are each of you comfortable with being here and engaging in a candid discussion wherever it may lead?"

No one immediately responded, smiling approval at the attorney general's remarks, perhaps not sure where the discussion might lead.

Governor Simmons quickly interjected, "Thank you, Della, for breaking the ice...as usual, you are right on time and target." He smiled and continued, "Let's all take a seat and relax; more wine anyone?"

To this point they had all been enjoying casual conversation. Each maneuvered around to one of the comfortable leather upholstered chairs which faced inward to a large glass top coffee table; no one moved to refill their glass at the elaborate mahogany bar where there were open wine bottles stood; one each of chardonnay and cabernet.

"My friends permit me to proceed from the point where Della acknowledged our presence here," Simmons continued as he settled into a chair at one end of the coffee table. "A lot of things have been going on in my head before and especially during these few days I have been governor of this great state. My concern is for Texas, nothing more, nothing less, and for our great nation as well, of course. But importantly what we in Texas must do as certain political realities are coming more and more into play. Over the past few days, I have had the pleasure of chatting with each of you, especially Chris and Tom; mainly to get to know you better and a sense of your feelings about the state of the nation. I have also come to know that each of you here is a traditionalist, if not conservative and I am proud to be in your company. It is clear the democrats now have this country under their control; nothing short of a miracle will give us an opportunity to stop their various social legislative agenda. I am aware the sort of talk we are venturing into may appear impulsive and too close on the heels of my just assuming the office of governor, but I want to take advantage of the presence of our Texan military leaders and want to hear from each of you to the extent you are comfortable with this format. I believe that all of us recognize that 'change' is here and more is coming and it will alter the landscape of the entire United States."

Some grinned at Simmons enunciation of the term "change."

"The critical question for all of us," he continued, "is how we can, or more importantly, should we at this time, respond? Would it be better to wait for another general election with the thought that republicans may regain full control of congress? If so, would they have the gumption, strategy, and power to mitigate the president's agenda? If we were to act now, what specific legislation, laws or state prerogatives can I use to counter their liberal agenda to protect and keep Texas and Texans from continuing to be forced to accept these unwanted liberal and socialistic changes? I need your wisdom and guidance in this matter."

"Before we proceed," he paused, smiling as he held up the palm of his hand toward Della Murphy who appeared eager to respond further, "with our discussion permit me to add to Della's remarks, we are in confidential and secret dialogue here; everything is off the record and no notes should be taken. I am open to any of your comments and thoughts. Oh, and let me ask," eyeing Chris Mitchell, "are you headed back to Washington promptly or will you be in Austin for a few days before returning?"

General Mitchell responded, "Governor, thank you for your confidence and candor, and for inviting us to this gathering. I can share with you and I am sure that Tom Lawhorn will confirm, that the two of us, among others, have had a few discussions relative to the consequences of the last presidential election and frankly we are concerned for the dramatic turn this country is taking under the democratic party leadership. Just about every day, we get new requirements from the White House and other government agencies. During my time in military service we have never had such a politically oriented defense department and many senior military officers have a growing anxiety with this. When this in combined with a congress and president who are bent on taking this country down a path which I believe none of us in this room desires, in fact may fear, we must consider alternatives and I believe the time to do this is now! With regard to me personally engaging in serious talks about the future of our nation and state, I am coming up for retirement in a couple of months and matter of fact, I am job interviewing while I am here in Texas anyway. So, yes, I would be pleased to stay in Austin for a few days longer or whatever time it takes for us to talk some of this out."

Mitchell's remarks were interrupted by a knock at the door and Governor Simmons responded, "Ah that must be Manny Estrada. I invited him to come over; hold on a minute, Chris."

Gene Todd quickly rose from his chair, stepped over to the door and opened it. Manny Estrada nodded to Todd and entered the room.

"Mr. Speaker! Come in Manny," Simmons greeted. "I believe you know these folks or have met them over the past few days, please have a seat; glass of wine?"

Estrada shook his head with a cautious smile to the offer of wine, perused the assembly sitting around the coffee table, proceeded to verbally acknowledge each, shake hands and sat down in the remaining empty chair saved for him.

"Go ahead General Mitchell," Simmons continued. "You were about to say..."

Chris Mitchell continued, "Mr. Speaker...Manny, good to see you again. That's about it for now, Governor, (not feeling quite the same as before Estrada arrived). I'll defer to the others for the time being."

"Thank you, General. Tom, what say you?" Simmons smiled and asked, looking at the national guard chief.

"Yes sir, I will be in Camp Mabry for a few days before visiting with various state guard folks at several bases throughout the state." General Lawhorn responded. "I see no harm in discussing the concerns for our state during these difficult times here and abroad. I share the many concerns of General Mitchell regarding the future of our national security and the democrat party's agenda for social change. To me, it is clear these issues are impacting our military and national security as well as our personal values. I have listened quite closely and I am firmly against their ideas of what they think is best for our country and I do not intend to be silent from my guard position...for as long you continue to appoint me to hold this position that is. We have never been burdened as heavily for guard deployments in any previous wartime situation. Of course, you all know the reason why...the previous democratic administration and his democratic congress decimated our active duty components during the nineties and we never fully recovered before 9/11. That has made it doubly hard on our guard and reserves. Like all of you, I am a fiscal and social conservative and a traditionalist whose heart and mind are embedded in the spirit of Texas."

"Good, thanks, Tom;" Simmons acknowledged.

"Governor, if I may," General Mitchell raised his hand to again speak. "Just to add to my previous comments, I have had numerous discussions with others in the Pentagon, both military and civilian, about the present and potential events occurring in the country and many share a growing disenchantment with not only what is happening to our national security and military readiness, but the dramatic social disorder this administration is bringing to all citizens whether they want it or not. My ancestors came to Texas over one hundred and fifty years ago and I love this state and I share each of your concerns with the mounting issues in the country and the democrats imposing their aggressive socio-political values on those of us who would not subscribe to such. As I see it, the challenge before us is to determine exactly what any of us can do to stop and or forestall any unwanted legislation or new and potentially hurtful political policies."

"Thanks, Chris," Simmons acknowledged. "I appreciate your candor and commitment. Rest assured we are all equally concerned about the values you mention and which we all cherish."

"I will just add," Mitchell said. "Permit me to suggest as we continue this discussion and perhaps others, that each of us exercise prudence in our thoughts and in particular our actions. Not one of us can afford to breach our respective official positions, particularly the two of us on active military duty. While we all love Texas and want to safeguard our people and remain cognizant of our special history, we must not jeopardize either in the process of seeking a remedy to the crazy changes coming from Washington, regardless of what they may consider to be 'good for the country.' Please know that I am amiable to supporting any and all rational and reasonable notions in that regard."

"Well said, Chris," Simmons responded. "Good advice. Manny, you've heard most of what has been said to this point; any comments?"

"Well..." Speaker Estrada hesitated. "Uh, yes sir, Governor. Thank you for inviting me, 'I think'..." he smiled, half frowning. "I can see you are in a very serious dialogue. I love my state as well, as several of you have expressed; that is without question. We have just concluded a turbulent special session which was intended to deal with one of the major issues confronting Texas and the nation at large; immigration and the thousands being killed on our border, of course. This is an issue that Washington has ignored. But, that is only one issue that is affecting the entire nation. I have been closely monitoring the various social legislative actions being promulgated by Washington and I do not like what I am seeing. Perhaps you have already spoken to some of the others, in particular economics, which in my view is very important. Although I will add, Texas is currently enjoying an enormous surplus in the "Rainy Day Fund," some 10 to 12 billion dollars, as compared to California, Massachusetts and Michigan, among others, with multi-billion dollar deficits. So before continuing, I should ask: what is this meeting all about, what is our agenda and what do you, Governor, want from each of us?" He continued "This is a very diverse group, state officials and U.S. military officers; where do we come together and for what purpose?"

"You have hit the issue square in the eye, Manny," Governor Simmons responded. "I invited each of you here because of the love for your state and seemingly congenial nature, but also for your respective professional backgrounds. Each of you brings exceptional personal qualities; combine those with your individual expertise to perhaps carry out an extraordinary and heretofore un-thought of stratagem to help keep Texas a traditionalist state."

The governor paused; the others were obviously reflecting on the comments that each had expressed and searching for conclusions to the discussion. The governor had listened carefully to each of the individual views. He was particularly impressed with the cohesion, sincerity and willingness on the part of the assembled group and felt secure that this very small sample of loyal Texans might just be the catalyst to assist him in addressing the future state of affairs which lay ahead.

The governor broke the brief silence, "Della, gentlemen, I am so pleased that we have had this opportunity to gather informally and briefly discuss some of the issues that face our nation and seriously impacting the serenity of the great state of Texas. I am very grateful to each of you. General Mitchell has alluded to it; we cannot breach our positions, but in observing and listening to each of you, it is abundantly clear as we deal with the policies coming from Washington that we must consider the potential downsides of the political future of our nation and our state, but with rational thought and judgment. But, this is not the time for rash acts and not knowing exactly the path that lies ahead, we must remain prudent. Perhaps as soon as our schedules permit I would like to arrange for another such informal meeting to continue this discussion."

"Attorney General Murphy," he continued shifting to an official tone. "Before we convene our next meeting, I want you to research the depths of our history and the Texas Constitution in particular, the historic times between 1836 and 1868, as well as 1871 and the conditions and legalisms that brought Texas back into the union. I want every constitutional law of the United States researched, especially the 10th Amendment, and dissected regarding the legal relationship Texas has with the United States government. In other words, what if any, are the constitutional and legal options that we can consider in countering the impositions of the 'change agenda' that is now upon us. Della, you must do this without any outside assistance; especially from your staff."

"Yes, sir," Della Murphy quickly replied.

Simmons turned his attention to a more informal tenor, "General Mitchell...Chris, Tom and for that matter, Manny...at the moment, I am not sure how each of you can interact or participate in this..." he paused, "wherever we are headed, but I personally value your friendship and allegiance to Texas and I wholeheartedly welcome whatever you can or are able to provide in thought or substance to any and all options that as individuals and as a team which we may consider over the next few weeks and months. We are all Texans here in this room and no matter what happens; I want us all to be proud Texans when all is said and done."

He took in a shallow breath; looked around for a brief moment, "Well, that's it for now." He was clearly fatigued; his voice reflected the strain of the fast pace following Shahan's sudden death, his own prompt inauguration, the funeral service and finally this hastily called meeting.

"Before we plan to gather again," he continued. "I would ask each of you to explore and think about various measures which we might consider. Again, I want to thank each of you; I have kept you far too long particularly on this already long and arduous day of mourning Governor Shahan's passing."

Chapter Three

Governor Simmons had wanted to reconvene a meeting with the group promptly before Mitchell returned to Washington so as not to lose any momentum from the gathering. But the following morning, he realized that the press of details associated with the duties and responsibilities of assuming the governor's chair made it virtually impossible. He had quickly narrowed his candidates for lieutenant governor to three, two state senators and one member of the legislature. He called Della Murphy and Gene Todd over to his office.

"Della, I need your wise counsel," he said. "David Keenan, Harry Johnson and Daniel Stauffer...you pick," he smiled.

"Dan Stauffer," she replied without hesitation, knowing full well the subject. "You asked and you know me, I don't equivocate," she smiled. "Dan has served our state with distinction as a senator and budget and finance committee chairman," she continued. "He may be a little strident at times; I chalk that up to his youth and energy, but he is damned smart and will be an important player in our state and perhaps the country in the years to come."

"I can always depend on you, Della," Simmons smiled. "You have made your case; Dan Stauffer is my choice as well, but I wanted your cogent input. Thank you."

"Okay," he continued. "I'll call Senator Stauffer when we are finished here; I have little doubt he will refuse." They all grinned. "Della, as soon as I receive a response from Dan Stauffer, you may take it from there; we'll need to convene a special call session of the senate for a confirmation hearing so I will get in touch with the Senate Pro-tem. Gene, get a release ready, I will let you know as soon as Senator Stauffer accepts and we'll get this move done."

Senator Daniel Stauffer was a native of Fredericksburg and recognized as a "fast burner" in the state senate. He was a graduate of Harvard with a degree in political science. Following graduation he immediately got into politics thereafter; first elected to the State House and then to the Senate as soon as he became eligible. He had a reputation of being brash, frequently quick-tempered and engaging in conflict with colleagues, but also highly respected for his intellect and in being correct on virtually all issues. He was swiftly confirmed as lieutenant governor of Texas by a majority vote in a special call session of the senate.

The governor appointed Della Murphy as his de facto 'Chief of Staff' to orchestrate further coordination among the group he had hastily assembled following the funeral service. Della had a natural flair for the air of secrecy and enjoyed creating study groups. She established a secure communications network; assigning the code name, *Excalibur,* for the governor, "*Sixcom*" as the reference name for the planning group and arranged for special *Blackberry* smart phones to be provided to each of the members.

"This is not an absolute secure communication system," she advised the governor, "but we are netted within our group with special numbers and access codes, and we will use your code name when using the smart phone system. If it becomes necessary we can create code names for each of us, but for now I would like to try to keep it simple."

"Good start, Della," he responded, obviously pleased with her consistent efficiency. "Now to your research; you are going to require some additional support. Who do you have in mind?"

"Jacque Adams," she promptly replied. "You know her...my special assistant. She's my genius and secret weapon; we can rely on Jacque to do anything and do it right."

Jacque Adams had a law degree and was a scholar in Texas government and the constitution. She was thirty four years old and married to a legislative assistant to a state senator. After working with Jacque for almost three years, Della felt confident that she could trust Jacque with any task, no matter the complexity, she would produce.

"Good choice," Simmons smiled. "You're having fun with this aren't you," he chided. "Get to work and keep me posted."

"Yes, Sir," she smiled. "Oh, Sir, when do you want to bring Lt. Governor Stauffer in on this," she quickly added.

"Not now, Della," he replied. "He is busy enough learning his new job and I want to keep him focused there for the time being. I will advise him that you are engaged in some special work for me and that I will bring him in at a later date."

"Yes, Sir," she replied, recognizing not to question him further. The confident governor had his reasons.

Della was elated with her new assignment; a refreshing departure from the routine of her day-to-day AG duties. She informed the *Sixcom* Group that the governor couldn't possibly meet again until much later due to his official duties, but assured them that he was as energized as ever to proceed with the planning process.

"I am researching to the degree possible, the history and the law, and the precedent, if any, of such actions we might consider to exercise our independent rights, especially the various interpretations of the 10th Amendment" she cautiously told them. "For planning purposes, *Excalibur*, would like to convene a meeting of the *Sixcom* six weeks from this coming Saturday if each of you can make it to Austin."

Mitchell and Lawhorn each acknowledged that they could be in Austin on Friday evening before and meet on the following day and Sunday as well, if necessary.

"Good," Della acknowledged. "I don't need to suggest you travel anonymously, but I know you will. I will also arrange for a 'special' car and driver to meet you General Mitchell and drive you to the Fairmont Hotel where reservations will be in your names. General Lawhorn, I will assume you will drive your own car from Camp Mabry. Unless there is some change, we will plan to hold our meeting somewhere here in Austin; in all likelihood where we met previously; I will let you know."

Della Murphy convinced the governor that they needed to expand their *Sixcom* to include other constructive members. Trusting her judgment, he agreed and she proceeded to visit with Alexander Mason, an African-American state representative from the legislative district southeast of Houston. She knew Alex Mason well; he was a lawyer, a conservative democrat, married with three children, very bright and good friend whom she trusted as a law partner in their earlier days. She also knew that while he harbored certain prejudices from his childhood, he could be trusted and would be an objective sounding board.

With the governor's permission, Della also recruited Gordon Giles, a Texas billionaire, President and CEO of TEXPRO, the largest independent oil and gas production company in Texas. He had presided over the State Republican Party for several years in the past. She told Giles that the governor had requested he join a small group to review the State's energy policies as it applied to Homeland Security. Even with the innocuous tone of such a meeting, he became excited at the prospects of meeting with the governor and discussing Texas' future in light of the liberal doldrums that he so feared. Della then granted both Mason and Giles special commissions and assignment to the Office of the Attorney General which was routine for gubernatorial appointments.

Della and Gene Todd worked up a scenario for the next meeting of *Sixcom* that called for a homeland security forum hosted by the governor on the last weekend of November, to be held in the governor's office in the capital.

Todd issued a press release that characterized the forum as a routine periodic homeland security review by the governor and due to the potential sensitivity of certain matters which might be discussed; the media would not be included. Picking up on the homeland security theme, Della suggested to the governor that they drop the *Sixcom* name in favor of 'homeland security forum' as I believe we should call it like it is," she said. "After all, it is our 'security' and our 'homeland' that is at risk." The governor agreed.

The second meeting of the governor's homeland security forum convened at 9:00 a.m. in the same small conference room adjacent to the governor's office in the capitol building where they met previously following Governor Shahan's funeral. Della and Jacque Adams had briefly introduced them around and pointed out the coffee bar and facilities.

Governor Simmons entered the room after everyone else had arrived and shook hands with each of the principals, insuring that they had been served coffee or juice. After a brief bout of small talk, paying special attention to Alex Mason, chiding his old friend, Gordon Giles, asking Chris Mitchell and Tom Lawhorn about their well-being and if they had a pleasant trip, he motioned for them to take a seat in one of the comfortable leather upholstered chairs which were again had been placed in a circle around the over-sized coffee table.

The governor remained standing and began by introducing Alex Mason, Gordon Giles and Jacque Adams, and their respective positions. He then asked each of the group with the exception of Della Murphy, who everyone knew, to introduce themselves; nodding toward Chris Mitchell who was sitting closest to his left. Mitchell began and, in turn, each one provided a brief background about themselves.

"I am sure Representative Mason and Gordon are somewhat curious about the nature and purpose of our 'Forum' as Della has designated our group," Simmons began after each had spoken, "although I believe she has brought you briefly up to date, has she not, Alex?"

"Yes, Governor," Alex Mason replied, "but only to the extent that you wished to convene a group of individuals to discuss our state's well-being and future."

"Well, that's a good overview of our topic title, I suppose," Simmons frowned, perceiving that Della had not delved more deeply into their meeting purpose with Mason in order for him to expedite the proceedings.

"How about you, Gordon?" the governor asked.

"Sir, only briefly; that you wanted to get a group together to address our energy policies attendant to homeland security issues," Giles replied.

Della Murphy flushed; she had apparently misread the governor regarding how much she should discuss the details of this forum with the two new members. This was a most unusual situation for her; one who was always confidently at the top of her game. She quickly raised her hand.

"Sir, the lapse in providing more background to Representative Mason and Mr. Giles is my error," she said. "I apologize; I was not clear on how much you wanted me to discuss the issues before the meeting."

"That's okay," Simmons smiled. "Not a problem, Della; we have both been very busy these past few weeks and we look forward to your sharing all that you have researched for us. Well, let's begin and for the benefit of Alex and Gordon, I will briefly walk them through this swamp so to speak."

The governor continued to stand. "Some months ago on the evening following Pat Shahan's funeral, Generals Mitchell and Lawhorn along with Speaker Estrada, Della, Gene Todd and I met here in this room at my invitation. My purpose then, as it is now, is to ask you to assist me in assessing the state of affairs of our country and, in particular the state of Texas, in the aftermath of the national election held over two years ago. Without question, as conservatives I believe we all now feel the frustration, if not fear, that is bearing down on us as many believed the president and his cohorts have since caused an intolerable expansion of federal government intervention and authority over an individual state's sovereignty. I think I can speak for most if not all of you, this approach is totally unacceptable to those of us who appreciate each state and its right to autonomy, in particular when it comes to social and domestic legislative programs. He proceeded to name several of the social programs.

After a fairly comprehensive review, he paused for a moment, looked at his watch; "I'll just be another minute and then we can break for a stretch."

"Okay," continuing, "let me go to another serious issue. Our border to the south along the Rio Grande is out of control, as all of you know; El Paso is sitting on the verge of invasion by those trying to escape the rampant drug cartel havoc ongoing in Juarez. Illegal immigrants are flowing across the border at an unprecedented rate and the consequence is the growing impact on our medical facilities, schools and economy. The murder rate in towns on our side of the border increases daily and thousands have been killed on the Mexican side. Okay, so this administration inherited the border problem, it has been with us for far too long and the present administration has done little to address the problem. Nevertheless, I fear even more so that the folks in Washington are being even more passive, perhaps even benevolent to problem. This is born out when Arizona recently enacted a law to deal with the illegal issue by deporting those who break the law; instead of supporting it, the president and his attorney general sued Arizona to stop the law from being implemented. Not being deterred, Arizona is also trying to get a law passed denying automatic citizenship to children of those mothers who sneak across the border just to have them born in the USA. The administration is again saying no! These are strong signals that the feds will take action against any state that tries to deal with the problem of illegals. With this and other major issues being pushed onto us from

Washington they are tearing at the soul of Texans. The rhetoric bears out these folks in DC are trying to make us do and accept things that our momma would not like. If we do not find a way to prevent further actions, then we are in a heap of trouble as my daddy used to say." He paused and looked at his audience smiling, "okay, let's take a break. I don't want to wear you out with my oratory; walk around, stretch and we'll reconvene shortly."

They each got up from their chair, stretched and began individual conversations around the room.

Chapter Four

"Well folks, let's continue," Governor Simmons offered as they returned to their chairs after a twenty minute break. "You have listened to me ramble on lamenting about what I feel the concerns are for our country and especially our great state; I do not have all of the possible solutions or remedies and this is why I must rely on your counsel, so I would like to hear from you. For the benefit of Alex and Gordon, I am sure you are wondering why I invited two senior military officers to this discussion; you have had the opportunity to visit with them informally so let's let them speak. Would you go first, Chris?"

"Thank you, Governor," Chris Mitchell responded. "As Governor Simmons mentioned, this is our second such discussion concerning issues that confront our nation and state. The governor has characterized the concerns quite well, but perhaps first to the question, why am I here? Governor Simmons and I first met during the week of Pat Shahan's funeral. He, along with Tom Lawhorn, Della and I struck up a mutual friendship which led to his inviting Tom and me along with Speaker Estrada to visit with him following the services for Governor Shahan. As has been alluded to, we engaged in informal, but frank discussions. I am a Texan first, an American and an officer in the U.S. Air Force serving the country I love. I have fought in combat for the freedoms and way of life we have all come to comfortably enjoy and cherish. As the political campaigns began to unfold over two and a half years ago, I along with many of my colleagues began to wonder and question just what the collection of liberal democrat candidates had in mind as they slandered the incumbent republican president and his quest to take bold actions to defend the country from further attacks such as we suffered on 9/11. Now we have found out. This brings me to another very serious concern to add to the governor's list and that is national security. The president, amply supported by an enabling and co-opting media with their almost daily so-called poll taking, ramp up every issue, usually in order from one to four, to make clear what 'they' thought were the priorities most sought by the American people on a given day. You all know the litany; health care, education, economy and sometimes immigration, and frequently the list was flip-flopped or mixed around to suit the issue of the day. Not in one of those polls have I ever seen national security listed as a priority; I mean never at the top or the bottom, much less even a concern. Oh, and if Iraq or Afghanistan happened to be listed as a priority on someone's list, it was not done so as a threat to our national security, just the opposite; rather to ratchet up the 'get out and forget we were ever there crowd.' We are now seeing this approach to national security played out in Washington and I believe our nation is increasingly being placed in danger. Well, this forum isn't the place for an extended dialogue on that subject, although it is near and dear to me. Suffice to say, folks, without a national priority for security, not one of their so-called priorities count. Well, I have had the floor long enough; thank you, Governor."

"Thank you, General," Simmons smiled, "Well-stated. Let's see, we'll move around the group and hear from more of you; Mr. Speaker— Manny, would you like to share your feelings?"

Manny Estrada caught by surprise, looked up abruptly; he glanced around quickly and then slowly rose to his feet.

"No, no, Manny, keep your seat," Governor Simmons chided. "This isn't the gallery, so you can be comfortable."

The group chuckled.

"Thank you, Governor," Manny Estrada began. "Most of you know my background; I'm just a *wet back* ranch hand lawyer from the Big Bend country."

They all sniggered and some clapped their hands at his self-deprecating remark.

"And, I'm damned proud to be a Texan," he continued. The group all clapped again, welcoming the comic relief. "As speaker of the house, I find myself at a loss for words..." and quickly went on to speak, not wanting to make light of the serious discussion. "As the governor and General Mitchell have eloquently spoken, we are at a serious crossroad in our state and within the country. The actions taken by this administration and openly supported by those in the congress are alarming. I fear we have been exposed only to a glimpse of what they have in mind—'they' being the ones the president appointed to fill important cabinet and other special positions as well as two liberal supreme court judges to support him. The respective democrat congressional leaders are bad enough, but enough on personalities as we have our own here in Texas. Along with the governor, and I am sure most of you, I recognize the potential challenges, if not fear as I mentioned. But where do we go; where can we go? We are one of fifty states within the Union, locked-in by forty-seven on three sides and a foreign country to the south. A foreign country that is fraught with serious, if not critical, problems; economics, drugs, gangsters, political corruption as well as millions of good and decent people who seek peace and tranquility as do we. Mexico ranks eleventh in the world in population; that is no small issue facing Texas and America when the economy, education, health care, Iraq and Afghanistan amongst others and yes, General, national security as well, are added to the list. Mexico and the lawless border represent a threat to our state and national security. I have little doubt that what we have already seen as a precursor to their agenda may surprise us even more. It is clear that this administration is using their power to force their changes on us without constitutional authority and in many cases ignoring the 10th Amendment. What can we do? What should we attempt to do? I can't answer those questions. First, maybe we need to wait to see how the other conservative states respond to the president's social programs; thus far, except for the several states' attorneys general challenging health care reform, I have mostly seen acquiescence. Is it too early or too late to make any judgments or decisions about what we as a state can do? Second, if we do elect to take some actions, I believe we need to be cautious and very judicious in our considerations. Thank you, Governor."

"Thank you, Manny, excellent," Simmons nodded. "Well, I believe we can now break for an early lunch; Gene, Jacque, are we going to dine in here or do we relocate?"

"Sir, we are going to take a short walk to the private dining room," Jacque Adams responded.

"Good, show us the way, *Jacq*," Simmons smiled.

After lunch, the group settled back in the conference room, Governor Simmons continued with the series of round table comments. "I would like to resume our discussion and ask the others of you to briefly provide us your thoughts as General Mitchell and Speaker Estrada shared with us this morning. It is Saturday afternoon, so I will ask you to keep your remarks brief and hopefully we can get out of here before it's too late in the day. Let's hear from industry; Gordon would you mind sharing your feelings about the 'state of the state' with us?"

"Sure, Governor," Gordon Giles eagerly responded, quickly leaning forward in his chair; he then straightened up, eased back confidently, stretched out his long legs revealing the uppers of his expensive cowboy boots below his trouser cuffs. The flag of the Lone Star State was engraved in full color on the front of each boot.

"Thank you for inviting me here, Governor," Giles began in a measured drawl. "This is a most interesting get together—always good to see you; congratulations again on becoming our state leader, although we all regret the circumstances! Well, first, I am honored and fascinated with meeting all these new friends and what they have to say. Ditto to th' remarks by the General and the Speaker! They are right on the mark with my feelings. My business is oil and gas seismology and production to keep Texas and this country running, of course, but if I had my way I would go up to DC and clean out that whole damn mess in the congress, then go over to the White House and tell this liberal, socialist oriented guy to stop the nonsense! Since this last presidential election I have become so frustrated that I want to puke every time I hear the word 'change'! Change WHAT for crying out loud? Well, you all didn't invite me here to rant as I did enough of that over lunch, so forgive me. Honestly, folks, I don't know where we can go from here; we're stuck with this president fella and his go-along congress buddies like it or not for at least two or more years unless we wake up and throw some of 'em out. The liberal groups are powerful and well organized to insure this president gets elected to another term and that is something that would be difficult for me to accept. Our 43rd president was 'not their president,' well; let me say loud and clear: this guy ain't my president! As far as my input to your meeting here, I don't have any quick solutions that would be lawful, if you know what I mean.

I was up in the north central counties where I have four rigs working the Barnett Shale fields over there; which, by the way, that discovery has become a real asset to Texas. There is enough natural gas spread throughout that part of the state to carry us for no telling how long—that is, if this 'change' president doesn't decide to come down and take control of it like it appears he has in mind with his share and share alike philosophy; or, impose a mega-billion energy tax on our oil and gas revenues; this would kill the independents like me who produce the majority of the petroleum products in Texas and for that matter, the country! That also goes for the wind energy generation farther out west around San Angelo, Big Springs and Snyder; I'll bet we now have well over a thousand fans out there making electricity while those Yankees up in the northeast don't want 'em because they say they will destroy their precious natural environment. Environment, hell, they just want somebody else to do it for 'em and give it to 'em for free...spread the wealth; socialism at its best, I say!" Giles took a deep breath and sighed as he gazed around the group circled around him. "I'm open to any and all suggestions from you folks who are a lot smarter than me. Okay, nuff from me, Governor; thank you, sir."

"Thank you, Gordon," Simmons smiled. "Boy, nothing holds you back!" They all chuckled. "Okay, Alex, after listening to all of these eloquent expressionists, you must be warmed up by now," he smiled. "Would you care to share your thoughts with us?"

Alex Mason had sat quietly throughout the day, listening intently, likely attempting to assess the various viewpoints each of which centered on the directions the administration in Washington have been taking the country and that Texas is being penalized more than most because of its natural wealth, resources, and its traditional culture. Looking as well-groomed as he did when he first arrived in the morning; dark pin-striped suit, silver neck tie, pocket handkerchief to match, he sat up straight and acknowledged the governor's invitation, nodding with a polite smile.

"Thank you, Governor," Mason began in a soft voice. "First, I am honored to be included among this exclusive group of patriots. This is a most interesting and informative day. I have also been wondering

31

where I fit among these various thought processes. Black people have been a part of Texas culture since the beginning. I've heard it said, 'if you're a real Texan—be you brown, black, white, yellow or red—you don't rightly belong anywhere else'. That fits my ancestors and me. While we have had our share of racial problems, to me, there is nothing more important than believing in the values and pride that comes with being a Texan. I have a concern whether my children will have the same exposure to traditional values and morality as I did growing up. I share most of the comments I have heard spoken here today, but perhaps I am also an optimist. Governor, I don't believe that I can add very much to that which has already been said; perhaps later after I have digested it some. But, sir, I do have a question: I'm wondering about your true purpose for this forum. You have assembled and held meetings with an interesting mix of important people; two military generals, our attorney general, speaker of the house, an oil executive...yourself, the governor of our state. I understand that perhaps it's an opportunity for expressing displeasure with the impact of this president's agenda, but what is your expectation and what might you anticipate that this group or our state, for that matter, can do about influencing or changing any of the president's programs?"

Simmons smiled, "Alex, you have asked the critical question; what can we do as these fiscal and social programs of the administration continue to negatively impact on our state as several, including myself, have identified? Before I was inaugurated as governor of Texas, and throughout the last presidential campaign, I had my concerns with what I was hearing; I discussed them with Governor Shahan. Both he and I shared a common anxiety as we observed and listened. It became clear to us that the man who became the President of the United States expressed interest in introducing and implementing radical ideas and programs that have now become a direct threat to the well-being of America...Texas, in particular will suffer. As Abraham Lincoln once said, 'Out of suffering, there comes a new birth of freedom.' And let me be perfectly clear, if we fail to act the people of Texas will most definitely suffer as more and more social and spending programs take place. That is a long-winded response, Alex, but to the core of your question, I don't know what or how we can begin to address the future. That is why I invited you among a cross-section of bright, perceptive and thinking people to join me in deliberating the now and the potential future of Texas."

The governor, trying to contain his slight irritation, continued, smiling. "As to what can we do, as you say, to stop, prevent, or influence the president's programs, likely very little; the question is what can we do to safeguard or hedge against the potential over-burden of their programs on Texas?"

"Yes, sir," Mason responded. "I am just wondering if perhaps we shouldn't exercise a bit more patience with a man who has yet to complete his full term as president. Thank you, sir."

"Thank you, Alex," his lips pursed, smiled. "I sincerely appreciate your thoughts; that is why we are here...to exchange ideas and views. Well, General Lawhorn," he said, shifting his attention. "Would you care to share your thoughts with us?"

"Yes, Governor, thank you," Tom Lawhorn acknowledged. "Sir, this has been an interesting exchange," he began. "And, no doubt we are experiencing dramatic changes within the country, perhaps more so than in any past presidential successions. As several have already expressed, there are numerous concerns that have evolved and continue to do so since the election. It is now become more than 'it's the economy stupid;' it is the economy along with national security, immigration, deficit international trade, education, health and human services, increasing welfare benefits, and most important to me— the outright assault on our Texas traditions and our culture and I could go on, but you have more than adequately covered each of these issues in significant detail. I am not a politician, although I am your appointee and my posting as head of the Texas National Guard Bureau is at the pleasure of you, governor, and it will end when you say so. However, as is the normal course of such expected appointments, I will want to retire before too long. That would provide me with a new lease on life, so to speak, and free to express my opinions even more to you and others who are worried about the future of Texas.

I suppose, governor, my principal concern as already expressed by General Mitchell is national security and what their social changes will do to our Texas traditions; without the assurance of security over our homeland, especially Texas with its long border with Mexico, these other issues mean very little to us. While our guard and reserve resources are stretched more so than ever in history, we must persevere. I will criticize the current administration for allowing this to happen—there was adequate time and resources even in spite of the ongoing war in Iraq and Afghanistan to rebuild the regular military forces from the debacle of the past post-cold war downsizing by the previous Washington crowd. That's history and here we are now experiencing another 'peace-loving' appeasement pack in Washington. Well, there's not much we Texans can do about that. Perhaps our focus should be on fighting against the numerous social changes that are being downloaded onto us without a concern as to whether we want these changes or not. So, you invited us to come together and talk about the potential, if not the reality, of these changes that's been brought on for our country, but I am just not sure what I can offer to avert the inevitable, as ominous as it seems. I will make mention of one troublesome change and that is the don't ask, don't tell policy which is being eliminated; in my opinion, this will impact on the effectiveness of our military forces for years to come. Another program that is clearly against my grain is gay marriage and these are things that I cannot accept as being a constitutional right. As a military officer, I would have serious doubts that I could defend the United States on such."

Lawhorn sighed and continued. "So, Governor, without proposing anarchy," he shrugged and smirked, "when it comes to legal opposition to this administration, I am as much at loss as I believe the others are. Thank you, sir."

"Thank you, General Lawhorn," Simmons replied, his face outwardly expressing concern as to what his next move should be. "Let's take a break," he said abruptly. "Della, Manny, Gene, would you join me in my office, please?"

"Folks," Simmons began with the three standing before his desk. "First, I am pleased with the free expression of each of our guests; we have a good cross-section and mix of ideas—or, I should say anxieties. So, see if you agree with my thoughts: the holidays, Thanksgiving and Christmas are coming up, the administration will continue to bring on new programs no doubt many of these will be in regard to more social changes, the economy, banking, housing market, illegal migration control—or, the persistent lack thereof and so on. Therefore, I am suggesting we conclude this forum and plan to reconvene in mid-January before the start of the new congress and further assess the situation. What say you?"

"Governor," Della began. "As much as I would like to move faster and decide upon a course of action for our state, I agree that we can conclude this meeting for now, continue to monitor national and world events as this administration deals with international and domestic issues, but I do not believe that we should coast and wait for the other shoe to drop. I would like to continue full steam ahead with my constitutional research and prepare a contingency plan for yours and the forum's consideration. In brief, sir, I am frightened as hell."

"Thanks, Della," Simmons smiled at her unrelenting verve. "Absolutely, continue your course of action and keep me posted along the way. Manny?"

"Sir, as I previously expressed, I agree with a steady as we go approach," the speaker replied. "I really believe we need to assess where this Washington group is headed next; however, if something drastic is put forth that poses an immediate threat to Texas that would be a cause for concern on our part, we may have to move quicker. Between now and our next meeting we must keep our antennae to the winds of Washington and be prepared to meet sooner if needed."

"Good point, Manny. Okay, that's it for now," Simmons nodded. "Della, by all means continue along the pathway we have discussed; Gene, you can release a tepid report of our homeland security forum, no names of those in attendance and keep the whole event low key so as not to prompt questions—you know the ruse."

"Okay," Simmons nodded. "Let's go back in, I will close out the meeting and invite them to the mansion for informal cocktails." he smiled. "It's too late to set up dinner there; Gene would you call my wife, alert her to my impulsive gesture and make arrangements for our group to socialize for an hour or so at the mansion and then to dine in a private room at the Four Seasons."

Simmons reentered the conference room with Della Murphy and Manny Estrada in tow. "Folks, it's getting late and I'm sure you are about as drained as me," Simmons began. "I believe that we have had a good day of mutual exchange, so I would like to adjourn for now and plan for a follow-up session after the holidays. I have asked Della to schedule a meeting along around mid-January; in the meantime, I ask you to reflect on the various views expressed today and if you can rejoin us in January we will continue the discussion. Between now and our next meeting, I implore you to keep coming up with ideas on how we can respond, offset, deny, the unwanted changes coming from the president and his congressional cohorts. Now, I want to invite you to join me and my wife at the mansion for an informal social hour and then to the Four Seasons for a relaxed dinner. I know this is impromptu, but I hope that you all can join us."

Chapter Five

Della planned and coordinated a meeting of the *forum* for the weekend of January 26th. They would meet at the Shoreline Hotel in the Lakeway resort community, some 25 miles west of Austin. Feeling somewhat confident, Governor Simmons invited Lt. Governor Dan Stauffer and Zach Hollis, Director, Texas Department of Public Safety, to join in the meeting.

Chris Mitchell arrived from Washington on Friday evening of the 25th and was met by an aide from the governor's staff who drove him to the hotel at Lakeway. Tom Lawhorn drove his own vehicle to Lakeway from the Ft. Worth Joint Reserve Base where he had been visiting, arriving shortly after General Mitchell. The two officers met in the hotel lounge shortly after their arrival, enjoyed a few drinks and awaited further instructions about the meeting.

Della Murphy, along with Gordon Giles, Alex Mason and Jacque Adams arrived around eight p.m.; Della led her entourage along with Mitchell and Lawhorn to a private conference room on one of the hotel upper floors. Jacque Adams had pre-arranged for dinner to be served in an adjacent dining room. Governor Simmons arrived around eight-thirty with Speaker Manny Estrada and Director Zach Hollis. Lt. Governor Dan Stauffer and Gene Todd followed in a separate vehicle driven by a state trooper.

They joined the others in the dining room where they were finishing their dinner. Simmons introduced Lt. Governor Stauffer and Zach Hollis to the others. "We had a snack before departing Austin," Simmons told the group. "Please finish your dinner and we'll join you for dessert and coffee."

After dessert was served and the wait staff had departed, the governor said, "Manny and I briefed Zach on some of the preliminaries during the drive over and will leave the nitty-gritty to that which evolves in the process of our discussions. As you know, Zach not only heads the State Highway Patrol Troopers, but the Texas Rangers as well. I will leave the details of his responsibilities as we proceed.

If you all are wondering how I was able to escape from my office to come out here," he smiled, "Lt. Governor Stauffer and I are attending a 'homeland security conference retreat' as far as my office and any others are concerned. Two of Zach's trusted troopers drove us out."

The governor then looked around the room, observing his charges. "Della," he smiled, "it appears you have assembled all of our team; well done! So, I suggest that when you have finished your desserts we might order an after dinner aperitif, relax, visit for short while and then get down to business in the morning. Do any of you have questions for now?"

The homeland security forum had now grown to ten as they relaxed in an adjoining lounge with the new members getting to know each other. After an hour or so of socializing, the governor announced he was going to turn in for the night and would look forward to seeing them at 7:30 for breakfast in the adjacent dining room.

Governor Simmons was up early and the first to arrive in the conference suite. He used this time to ponder. Soon, the others arrived. They gathered round the carefully prepared table, sipped coffee and chatted while the hotel service staff set up the breakfast buffet. Della Murphy promptly announced that breakfast was ready. She excused the hotel staff members and posted the state troopers who had accompanied the governor and Lt. Governor Stauffer outside the conference suite. Each member of the group proceeded to serve himself from the ample buffet. Conversation among the group while eating was minimal and light-hearted; most were absorbed in individual thoughts about what the day might bring.

"Okay, folks," Governor Simmons announced, breaking-up the breakfast chat, "let's all adjourn to the conference room; feel free to bring along your coffee with you, if you like. There will also be a fresh pot next door."

They all moved into the adjacent room and found comfortable chairs arranged in a large circle. A coffee, juice and water bar had been set up off to one side.

"Della," the governor grinned, "you always do it right; nothing to want for."

"Give all the credit to Jacque and the hotel staff, Governor," Della responded. "And let me mention that we are reasonably secure to carry on any conversation within this room. I had the Texas rangers shake it down yesterday; it has been locked and under guard ever since they completed their work. Lastly, Jacque will be documenting our discussions; there will no electronic recording, at least for this meeting; together she and I will do our best to accurately replicate the proceedings."

"Thanks, Della." Simmons responded. "Okay, let's get started. This is apt to be a long day, but we will try to wrap it up by nightfall, if not we can stay over and I promise we will very quickly do so in the morning. You have all had an opportunity meet and learn a little about each other. As you recall, at the conclusion of our last meeting I asked each of you to consider workable ideas and possible solutions to the challenges that face our nation and Texas, in particular. I know I was asking for a lot but I also knew that each of you would put forward your best efforts. In searching for possible solutions, it has always been our shared goal to try our best to work within our system of laws both for Texas and the U.S. constitution. As the day progresses, we want to keep in mind that it is the people of Texas who we are obliged to serve. I am eager to hear from each of you. Manny, why don't you start off the discussions?"

"Thank you Governor," Manny Estrada nodded with a weak smile. "Since we last met I have experienced several headaches and heartaches. When I left you, I thought I would discover a wealth of resources and legislative support that would point to Texas having a way out of the new laws and social changes which, as we all know, we do not accept as being suitable for the people of Texas. I have spoken privately with each of our two U.S. senators, and with our congressmen, asking them for their guidance and what action, if any, they could take to mitigate the president's policies and help preserve Texas as a traditional and conservative state. Being part of the Washington establishment, it was not a surprise when not one of them had any suggestion whatsoever that would counter-balance the democratic agenda. It what's to come that worried me as I chatted with and quizzed each one.

The few members of the Texas senate and house with whom I have met are supportive of some form of resistance, yet none spoke of a solution. The friends who I have counted on for years when facing political and social problems are much like me, in a state of anxiety and fearful of the future, especially if the president gets elected to a second term. Craig Cabot, my lifelong friend who now heads up the Ranchers Association is in a state of disgust over the president's actions and their smacking at those who hold traditional values. In my discussions with these people it was clear that they are 'fired up' and are counting on Texas leadership to take on this challenge and put a stop to further changes coming from Washington. If I had to summarize their feeling which I have come to accept as my own, it would be a hopeless one hanging on to the question of 'what can we do to prevent liberalism and its partner socialism from continually being shoved down the throats of Texans?' Can we count on the supreme court? It is extremely doubtful, as there is not one single southerner, especially a Texan, who is now a member or will ever become a member of that elite 'intellectual' group. Governor and colleagues, I wish I had a more favorable report to give, but that is about all I can offer at the moment."

"Thank you, Manny;" the governor was quick to respond. "I appreciate your sincerity and the effort you put into this. This is a new and evolving era in the history of Texas with dramatically new challenges and forces coming at us so strong they are wrecking havoc on our entire culture, character and history of our great state. It is clear that this administration is using controversial legislation and newly constructed laws to attempt to make us what we as Texans are not. It also clear that little or nothing will be done about our border situation with Mexico.

"While Manny's remarks are somewhat muted, perhaps more so than mine," he smiled. "Some of you have no doubt come up with some creative ways in which we can challenge Washington. Alex, how about you...?"

"Thank you, Governor," Alex responded in an obvious demurred tone. "As Manny mentioned, this has been a trying time for me as well, one filled with hope, doubts and even fear as the president and his administration go about controlling and changing the United States. While I initially wanted to give the president the benefit of doubt, I can tell you straight forward that I am dissatisfied with how things have evolved, especially with those who were appointed to key positions in his cabinet, especially the justice department, and throughout his administration. I also do not like the ongoing rhetoric in favor of homosexual marriage and promoting and legitimizing a welfare state, which I believe to be a scourge of the poor, especially blacks, to an even greater evil than it is now. There are other Washington driven issues that I also find difficult to imagine including strategic moves to centralize more power in the White House under a 'new star' type personality who happens to be our president. I also do not like the reality that far too many decisions and rulings coming from Washington and the courts are specifically designed to satisfy the phony East Coast intellectual superiority and the decrepit moral inferiority of the Hollywood West Coast, thus slapping down just about every traditional belief any black, brown, yellow, or white conservative might have. With this, diversity has taken on new meanings and has completely shifted from the thought of correcting some racial, gender, and economic imbalances to one so all-encompassing that if one elects to oppose such they are called a bigot or homophobe. I don't like this and neither do my friends. Enough said for now about this.

"As a part of my search for proposals to counter balance these and further dramatic cultural changes coming from Washington, I have counseled with several of my key constituents, church leaders and my family—all of whom happen to be black, in an attempt to determine their concerns. Yes, there were questions by a few as to how and why I would even question the administration of our first black president. I clearly remember one remark made by a good friend of mine that particularly struck a nerve; he said, *'Alex, you will be thinking like a modern day slave if you become a part of this hate movement against our first black president. Why are you even thinking that way? Why don't you especially and the country give this man more time?'*

"My response to him was clear. I said to him: I would rather be a slave to my Texas traditions and a great conservative cause that recognizes my dignity as a human being and a man whose heritage is soaked in the blood that has fallen from Texans who believed in something greater than themselves than be a slave to a liberal, weak, misguided president who happens to be black. Folks, I have the utmost love for Texas and the historical role it has played. You wouldn't know this but my great-great grandfather was a black man named Joe who served and fought with Colonel Jim Bowie during the siege of the Alamo. He could have left Colonel Bowie's side, but he didn't. and as we move forward, I will not leave your side and my station and forgo the duties that you may ask me to carry out. I know that there is something very special about being a Texan and like my great-great grandfather, I am prepared to defend our culture and our traditions. My love for Texas and its people far outweigh any black or racial duty which some liberals may feel I owe to them. It is definitely not about hating the president as I hate no one. During my election campaigns, I let my constituents know that I am a proud black Texan and they have reelected me each and every time. I will stay the course that best suits the history, traditions and aspirations of the people of Texas wherever that may lead. Governor that's all I wish to say at this time."

"Alex, your remarks struck a soft part of my heart," Simmons responded. "I truly appreciate your stand on this matter. I also want to thank you for your continuing support as we move forward. Let's take a short break and reflect on what we have heard. After that, I would ask Gordon to share his assessment with us; coffee time!"

During the break only small talk was exchanged between the members; each seemed to be caught up in their own thoughts. After Manny's and Alex's comments some likely felt the state was in a losing battle against the multiple transformations coming from Washington and their impact on Texans and their way of life.

As they returned to their chairs, Governor Simmons remained standing. "Gordon, it is your moment," he said smiling.

"Thank you Governor," Gordon replied with a determined expression. "I left our last meeting with an objective of making an assessment of the president's policies is having on the petroleum and other industries in the state of Texas. My view in one word: disastrous! I have spoken with several key business leaders throughout the state, many are good friends, and frankly, they are scared out of their wits with some even indicating they may move their business into Mexico or further south into Guatemala. Some strongly believe that the president, especially in his second term, will impose even further regulations on employee salaries, unionize their company and force them to hire only unionized workers because they would support the president. Small business owners feel that it is just a matter of time until they will have to close shop. Younger executives are now beginning to believe their chances of becoming a millionaire are slim to none. Some are concerned that stringent environmental and health care policies are making their business less competitive. New tax policies meaning higher taxes are just around the corner and are also threatening with many tired of their hard earned dollars going to Washington to support social programs they oppose. While many in Washington, and particularly in this administration, are at home with various types of socialism, Texas and Texans are capitalists at heart and will fight like hell to stay that way.

When asked what they were prepared to do to in the battle with Washington, most felt that the answers lie with you, Governor Simmons, and our state leaders. Their message to you is that they will support most any new measure or plan that prevents a socialist revolution. And I, as well, governor, am prepared to support you in any way, spend millions of dollars, if necessary, to fight this battle. I wish I had better ideas to present, rather than opinions. I will close by saying that I stand behind whatever action you and this group decides and I believe I speak for the majority of the business community of Texas. Thank you for listening and I look forward to hearing from the others."

"Thank you, Gordon. It is refreshing and reassuring to know that we have the support of the business leaders of Texas." Governor Simmons acknowledged. "Let's keep things moving along and hear from General Mitchell; Chris."

"Thank you, Governor," Mitchell responded. "Before I speak to the issue at hand, I just want to say how pleased I am to be sitting here with this fine group of Texans who are committed to keeping Texas, Texas. Tom Lawhorn and I have had the opportunity to discuss with you the various military and national security situations and their potential implications, so what I will be sharing with you today are further concerns that Tom and I both generally agree on. At the Department of Defense they are daily inundated with the president's team of bureaucrats primarily interacting with those senior political oriented officers who agree with their agenda and being generally dismissive of those who challenge them. Most of these power driven, presidential appointed people, have no military experience whatsoever, yet they are greatly influencing the direction and role of the defense department. It seems clear to many senior officers, and that definitely includes Tom and me, that in the near future the defense of our country is going to be greatly weakened. It is fair to say that this team seems to be more interested in the social side of the U.S. military than why we principally exist; gays having the right to marry and serve openly in the military, cutting the defense budget, scrutinizing veteran and retiree benefits, getting access to the records of past military tribunals with the thought of retrying some of those military personnel who were court-martialed long ago, and the largest issue...not dealing with our border drug wars. On top of this, the attorney general seems hell-bent on ensuring the military, FBI, and the CIA do not torture or otherwise intimidate captured terrorists by pouring water on their faces in order to get vital intelligence that helps protect our nation. Thus far, this department has not come up with a better plan to get needed information to help defend our homeland. Their initial approach was to bring terrorists to civilian trials. This was done in order to appease his political supporters thereby scaring the hell out of many who see this as a blunder and a direct threat to our national security. Happily, they have now changed their minds and are now having these prisoners tried at Guantanamo. When their social action programs are combined with the growing problem requiring our military and other agencies to be 'political correct' and thus overly sensitive to all religious and minority groups, in some cases, this is all done at the expense of national security. Many of our senior people are now afraid to act on critical intelligence information if it involves a risk of being political incorrect or if it makes reference to a particular religion. One could easily characterize those responsible for national security of our country as being timid and dysfunctional because of these restrictions.

"The vice president often appears to be mentally detached from critical security issues. before our recent mid-term elections the democratic speaker of the house, whom we shuddered, was third in line for the presidency and was considered a joke around the Pentagon. Had we found ourselves in a situation where the vice president, or especially the past speaker of the house became president, the United States would undoubtedly have been faced with unprecedented threats from terrorist actions, as the enemy is fully aware that these two individuals did not and do not have the foggiest idea of what it requires to lead a nation. I should add that conservative administrations have also had their share of ineffective leaders who occupied high positions of government. With our past mid-term election and the republicans gaining control of the House, we now have the opportunity to restore some confidence in the speaker's position. Republicans will also be in a position to challenge the president's national health program and other negative initiatives, if they have the courage to do so! Many feel that whatever the republicans do or try to do, it won't be sufficient to stop the president from going forward.

"Meanwhile, the administration is moving like wildfire to create friendly relationships with Cuba and Venezuela, both quasi-socialist dictatorships, apparently implying that the United States can learn something from these two renegade nation-states. Iran and North Korea are also being cozied-up to in grave hope that we can all *cumbaya* together. They believe that many defense dollars can eventually be redirected to support the president's socialist programs, thereby keeping more people on the welfare rolls and provide the votes to keep him and other liberals in office.

"I will be perfectly straight-forward with you," Chris Mitchell continued, "Our senior, war-tested generals and admirals are frustrated and aggravated to a boiling point. They would like to speak out to the American public, however, they all know what happened to the commanding general in Afghanistan when he spoke his mind to a reporter. It is a cardinal sin for a military officer, especially one of high rank and responsibilities, to speak out against a president and the administration. Consequently, morale is lower than any other point in recent military history and that includes the historical colossal political failure in Vietnam and the massive downsizing of our active duty forces at the outset of the Clinton administration. Tom and I both agree that this situation has created a growing and perilous national security danger that is causing many in the Pentagon to fear for the potential of what could easily open us up to the threat of a major terrorist attack—and sooner rather than later! There are several veteran generals who believe our vulnerability to a terrorist attack is even imminent, perhaps hitting the U.S. and several of our allies simultaneously. There is also major concern among these senior officers as to how or if the U.S. will respond when this attack occurs. Tom and I have personally spoken with several key generals who have made it clear that because of the perceived and anticipated confusion and disarray that would occur in the White House should such an attack take place, we as a nation would be paralyzed while our national leaders tried to figure out what to do...that the Department of Defense and the CIA would have their hands tied in trying to develop an effective response. It is my further contention that any internal political actions on the part of any state at that time would not be interfered with by the U.S. military. The country and the Washington crowd would be in a state of chaos and turmoil such as we have never known. It would amount to, I believe, *'every man for himself.'* Take from this what you may.

"Permit me to comment further, Governor, regarding the lack of confidence in the administration by our senior military leaders. Tom may want to add to what I am about to say. This eruption came at a time when the war and public support were at a critical stage, and changing of leadership has not improved the overall situation. This next year could be perilous, in particular, in the way the administration is conducting the war becomes more exposed, perhaps from Wikileaks releases; most Americans will likely say it isn't worth it...let's get out. With the political dynamics now found in Washington, these senior officers really have no choice, but to seemingly go along. This situation is one more example of the disarray, bordering on chaos, in Washington which is affecting even our most disciplined leaders. The main point here is more often than not, a military leader on the front line of a war is more capable and competent with national security than someone with *no* military experience sitting behind a big wooden desk back in Washington, particularly if there is a political agenda. Perhaps the analogy goes further with regard to the administration's decisions on a whole multitude of critical issues—immigration, national health coverage, economy and so on—by those who are least experienced to do so. Sorry, I got side-tracked, governor.

"I will wrap this up; as I have mentioned to you, I am retiring from the Air Force in a short while. I will be leaving Washington in a few weeks using my accrued leave to cover the remainder of my duty time.

I have bought a home outside of Ft. Worth and I intend to dedicate my time helping Texas survive this administration whether it be for the next two or four years under this anti-defense, pro-socialist, accommodating a *"can't we all just get along,"* president. Governor, I am at your service and will do my very best to assist you and the people of Texas. Thank you for listening to this pessimistic report; I wish I could be more positive. As someone who takes pride in our Texas traditions and our history, here in this beautiful state is where I take my stand and I am prepared to sacrifice everything for a cause that keeps Texans out of the wrap of socialism and a diffusion of our values. Before I turn the podium back, Governor, sir, may I ask Tom for his comments?"

"Thank you, Chris, that was an excellent discourse! Sure, by all means, I was going to call on General Lawhorn next. Tom, would you care to follow-up?"

"Thank you, Governor," Tom Lawhorn began. "And, thank you, Chris. You hit the nail on the head and, as you mentioned, I share every thought and comment that you have made. I, too, am prepared to give my all to defending the rights and obligations that we as Texans, and Americans for that matter, have in protecting our culture and our values. Unless there is a major change in the direction this country is headed by the end of this year, I will consider retiring from my role as your Texas National Guard Chief and settle into my homestead in McAllen. However, I do intend to stay on course and see our project through. During the past few days I have spent some face-to-face time with our Texas National Guard commanders. They are quite concerned that soon there will be orders from Washington to prepare for 'change" including another reduction in force. This president is apparently opting to reduce the size and strength of our military services while increasing the scope of welfare services. This is certainly on the horizon and national security will suffer. Many of our guard troops here in Texas are outright angry and are ready to dig in their heels. I know Governor Simmons understands the important role of our guard and will do everything in his power to stop anticipated negative actions. In summary, from a national security standpoint the next few months, perhaps years, do not look good for the United States and even worse for Texas. I would ask this assembled group to think and work hard to come up with possible counter-actions to what appears to not bode well for the country, or Texas. I believe there is no other choice other than a unified focus on what best serves the proud people of our state. I would like to make one more observation and that is under this president and his cohorts, we are rapidly losing our identity as to what it means to be an American. The latest theme is we are all one world village. In any event, and under no circumstances, will I permit him to take away my identity as a Texan. Also, I want to briefly mention this Wikileaks thing; the cyber channels are overloaded with material, sensitive and otherwise, revealing communications between Washington cabinet members and leaders at all levels along with senior embassy officials decrying the lack of confidence and competence in both our enemies and our allies. Say what we will about this Aussie fella' and his cohorts, and what their perceived agenda might be, whether he is doing the nation a disservice or not, the revelations are startling with regard to the agenda in Washington. Perhaps more on that later in our discussions. I thank each of you for your patriotism and especially you, governor, for your forbearance and courage.

"Thank you Chris and Tom," the governor acknowledged rising from his chair, "for a very candid and critical assessment of where we stand regarding the national security of the nation, or the potential lack of it, which appears to be evident under this administration. As I listened to each of your comments, I felt a sense of betrayal with the outright peace at any cost approach that is now being the dominant philosophy in Washington. The forlorn look on the faces of Manny, Alex, Gordon, Zach and Della while listening to you said more than anything that we must act to do something, and we will! Before hearing from Dan and Zach, let's take lunch break for an hour and a half to ponder what we have all heard from our colleagues. Della, Jacque, I am sure you have made exceptional arrangements for lunch. Thank you, each of you, and we will reassemble back in here at 2:00 p.m."

All but Lt. Governor Dan Stauffer rose from their chairs and proceeded to the dining room. He remained seated, seemingly in deep thought. No one appeared to notice as the door closed leaving him alone. He had listened intently and most of the individual comments were of considerable interest. All of this was essentially new information since he had not been previously brought into the discussions until this week when the governor mentioned some aspects of it to him. To that extent, he felt left out and ill-prepared to interact in the discussions, if not mistreated by the apparent oversight. His German ancestry frequently showed through when he felt colleagues were diverting information from him. Stauffer was a first generation Texan; his parents emigrated from Germany before he was born and instilled within him a strong Arian culture. His fellow senators held great respect for his astute quick mind; they also had learned to 'walk around' him on issues where he was steadfast in the negative to the position of others. Simmons had chosen him as his lieutenant governor for his exceptional brilliance and ability to make quality assessments, good judgments and decisions favorable to the state of Texas and the well being of its people. Stauffer was apparently trying to process what he had heard and reevaluate his early opinion. He was surprised that Governor Simmons had called upon him to make comments to the assembled group, especially since this was his first exposure to what he believed some fairly radical political assessments. He knew he had to respond in an intelligent, but also rational manner when the governor called on him within the next hour or so. After a few minutes, he quietly joined the others for lunch; thoughts from the morning's rapid-fire commentary continued to linger within him. It was not at all clear in his mind what all of this meant. He listened to the small talk and comments from others during lunch and did not participate. He was preoccupied with what, on this short notice, he might contribute intellectually to the discussion.

Chapter Six

The lunch break went quickly and the group reassembled and took their seats. Governor Simmons began the session.

"Now that we have full stomachs and cleared our minds somewhat, (there were a few chuckles which he acknowledged with an approving smile) I would like to restart the deliberations. I am well aware that this is his first exposure to these discussions; I mentioned them to him only a few days ago without considerable detail. After all, stepping into the lieutenant governor's chair on such short notice has kept him extremely busy. However, recognizing his unique ability to assess quickly and not wishing to embarrass him at all, nevertheless, I would like to ask Lt. Governor Dan Stauffer to offer us his impressions of what he has heard thus far...including his opinion regarding what he believes is happening and what we might expect to evolve in and from the Washington arena in the future. Dan, would you please share your thoughts?"

Dan Stauffer rose from his chair. "Thank you, Governor," he replied, nodding soberly. "My initial impression is that I am somewhat overwhelmed with what I have heard this morning, although I admit some of the points seem to be not far off from what I have been thinking. While I do not have the military, legal, or political experience that you all bring to the table, I am trying to understand your reasoning and concerns. The only thing I can possibly think of at this point is what and how can I provide support to the governor who I trust to make the best judgment on what actions we can take that are feasible, legal and workable. I am honored, sir, that you have asked me to be part of such a dedicated group of people who are as patriotic as I have ever seen. While I am eager to learn more, as of now, sir, you can count me in and I will endeavor to be a contributing member of the team."

"Thank you, Dan," the governor was quick to reply; we are pleased to have you on board. "Let's keep the ball moving and I want to turn to Zach Hollis; Zach would you honor us."

Zach Hollis remained seated and scanned the faces of the group before speaking. "I have served in law enforcement for nearly thirty years in several different capacities and I tend to evaluate things from that angle. I have never witnessed such a lawless situation as we have evolving in several of our Texas border cities. I am referring to the major incidents along the Mexico border. If the administration continues to make moves to allow amnesty and keep the individual border states from taking action as they did in Arizona, it's going to get worse with more drug peddling and killings occurring. Several of my friends in law enforcement and family members have been murdered by these drug gangs and cartel members.

"I have been told that the U.S. Attorney General is already working a plan to eliminate the right for people to bear arms; this irresponsible action will never be accepted by the people of Texas and most certainly not by me! Attendant to that anticipated ruling, there has been a rush across the state to buy firearms. That in itself is a frightening specter. Two border agents were brought to court a few years ago for shooting a drug dealer before he had a chance to shoot them. And as you know, these two agents were sentenced to prison for several years. The president's appointee for Immigration and Customs Enforcement, (ICE), has been sending signals that a new policy will soon be initiated to the effect, if we arrest an illegal we must document his presence and then let him go free. This is not my style of law enforcement, justice, or the law of the land to which I have dedicated my life. Clearly, I am not pleased with what I see unfolding; neither are my law enforcement colleagues. I recently discussed the crime situation in our state with several of my senior officers in the Highway Patrol and the Texas Rangers. They are all on board to accept the direction from the governor to curtail these illegal operations and to maintain order throughout Texas. They all asked me to tell you, Governor Simmons, you can count on them for their full support in any action you wish to take. Thank you, Sir."

"Thank you, Zach, and please convey my appreciation to those officers for their support," Simmons replied. "I will try not to let them down. Let's take a thirty minute break and then I will ask Attorney General Murphy to sum up for us."

The members stood, stretched, looked at their watches, and a few headed for the bathroom. Della was going over her notes to rekindle her information and from a lawyer standpoint make a good case to her jury. Shortly, she called the governor behind closed doors for a snapshot of how she would present her assessment. The governor was exceptionally interested in how she was going to wrap up this meeting and her final recommendations. Della took direct aim at the overriding issue on the table along with the additional considerations.

"Governor," Della began with her typical no nonsense approach, "after what we have heard from our various members during these several meetings, if it isn't clear to you what I see and acknowledge as well as what I believe is an imperative, then I don't know you as well as I think I do."

The governor looked directly at Della, smiling. "Fire away, counselor, let's see how close we are. Give it to us straight."

"Governor," Della began, "there is no need for me to go over in detail that which has been said and repeated at this or the other meetings. The political situation in Washington has without precedence created a threat to our national security, our Texas culture, values, traditions and our historical role in the quest for and sustaining our freedoms. I have examined every law and piece of legislation within our state as well as in the federal sector. There is nothing legally under states' rights provisions that we can wave before the world and simply tell Washington and this administration to 'stop it', get the hell out of our lives and let us govern the people of Texas civilly and peacefully. I believe we are down to two options; the first is simple, give into the extraordinary dangerous whims and demands of this administration and let things fall where they may. As I listen to you and our members, this option is unacceptable. Sir, with considerable deliberation and forethought, the other option reaches to the depths of radical reactionary conduct, but you have charged me with the duty to guide you. The office of attorney general, the people who elected me and especially all of the Texans who have put their lives on the line for our freedom also guide me." She paused; remained sternly focused while her eyes teared.

"Governor, the only viable option which I believe we have in my opinion is to declare secession from the United States and create an independent republic. Within our Texas Constitution, I can interpret that we have, again in my opinion, retained the right to secede if we so

53

choose. That is about as direct as I can state it. But, I must caution there are legal scholars who will challenge a secession declaration. They will argue that we gave up that right when we rejoined the union after the Civil War. I am prepared to challenge that argument, however."

Della smiled, wiping the tears from her cheeks, "In that you didn't flinched, falter or faint, and you're grinning, I suppose I didn't shock you too badly; perhaps you have already reached a similar conclusion?"

The governor pondered her remarks for a few seconds while Della regained her composure, shift from her own thoughts to where she would clearly hear while listening to him. "Della, I have known for some time that this option would probably be our only choice and it is one that without question is the most complex and difficult to accept. However, I have been over this time and time again; worried it, conducted my own constitutional research, reviewed our Texas history and I am now convinced this is our only option and I am prepared to see it through. Our past Governor Shahan during his final days even privately suggested to me that this may have to be our choice. There are many considerations, complications and details to work out with the implication, timing and supporting roles which we must rely on our assembled team to play—If they are willing? I feel strongly that most, if not all, will agree with our conclusion and participate fully in achieving the goal of a free, independent Republic of Texas. Della when we rejoin our members, I would like for you to summarize just the legal reviews and mention only the first option. I will then take it from there and suggest that I have an alternative option. I will announce that I have listened carefully to each of the concerns expressed and highlighted, conducted my review and with full confidence that secession is the only viable solution to the ills we face and I will ask their unwavering backing and support to go with me. Thank you, Della, for pointing us and the people of Texas in the right direction."

Della sighed and responded in a soft voice, "Governor, your decision to take Texas into a free republic is either the beginning of something noble and great for Texas or something that will potentially be our destruction. In either case, I do not believe we have a choice, we must take what I believe is this imperative step if we are to ever again look at ourselves as patriots and Texans! Sir, I am ready to move in the direction you choose and I believe God will be on our side."

"Let's roll!" responded the governor.

Chapter Seven

Governor Simmons followed Della as the members reentered the meeting room and took their seats. "Della will now share with you her findings and comments," Governor Simmons tersely began.

"Thank you Governor," Della responded, smiling. She scanned the assembled group, slowly making eye contact with each as if they were her jury. With a somber look, she began to speak with a strong voice. "I have provided the governor my findings and I will briefly sum up for you. Jacque and I have reviewed all the applicable laws and legislation in the Texas and U.S. Constitutions in an attempt to seek a way or means for Texans to challenge the president's many onerous programs.

"We are witnessing in this country social and political trends toward excessive central government control creating a type of nationalism unheard of since Hitler took power in Germany. While many do not see it this way, this over-zealous control by the government from my viewpoint is becoming more and more an accepted reality, intervening directly in our lives in ways that we in Texas reject. The election of this president has brought this certainty home more so than ever before. Centralization of power by the government, or nationalism, per se, has never been an issue with most Americans, or Texans, for that matter. We have been too busy enjoying our freedoms and special ways of life with little or no concern for losing them. Our founders thought of the United States more as a federation of states with individual rights than being tightly united, much less centrally controlled. It was that spirit and belief that persisted among those who brought Texas into the Union. Otherwise, they would have never traded their status as an independent republic for statehood.

"Nationalism includes the federal government controlling free market activities," she continued to fire up her jury, "is clearly at the root of bureaucratic power being placed over independent thought and action. It is a stepping stone leading to even more of a centralized liberal federal administration having a long held belief that this will give them what they have been wanting for years—socialism! If they achieve this goal, this will cause extraordinary operational expenses, which must be paid for and this means intrusion into the affairs of individual states with higher taxes, both individual and corporate, to support the growing bureaucratic glut. History reflects that nationalism has been at the core of initiating dissent and rejection for hundreds of years and perhaps it should not be any different this time. Texas has a rich and successful heritage of independence. We are the only state that was once a sovereign and independent republic. Texas fought its way out and from beneath the umbrella and shackles of a corrupt Mexican government to embrace nationhood. We now find ourselves in virtually the same familiar situation; our proud independent character, even our belief in God is being threatened by another national government located in Washington, D.C. and it slowly closing its grip on our inherent individuality, our traditions, and our culture. I believe that most Texans would once again fight to keep this from happening. But, as I have said, it's more than the potential loss of our individual rights, it is also the broad control of banks, businesses, industry, oil and gas enterprise, education, health care, you name it. This is what I fear most of this 'change' administration."

She paused, looked around the room, smiled confidently knowing that she had their attention, she continued to organize her thoughts. "Gentlemen, in reviewing the U.S. constitution, I am sad to say there isn't any constructive legal precedence or means that we have uncovered in this document that can help us refute what we will continue to see coming down the pike from Washington. However, in researching the Texas state constitution we just may have discovered a 'gem' on which we might make our case. I have briefed the governor on this one possibility. I am disappointed that I can't give you a more definitive report at this time. By each of us knowing the impact the Washington agenda is now having on the people of Texas, in law there is the term '*res ipsa loquiter*' which translated means, '*it speaks for itself.*' I have shared my professional opinion and personal views with the governor and I remain committed to support him in whatever action he may choose. Thank you, Governor."

"Thank you, Della," Simmons smiled. "I am pleased that I can always count on you. In digesting the content and meaning of Della's comments and opinions, and with respect to her legal findings, plus the candid comments coming from Generals Mitchell and Lawhorn and others, I believe we can narrow our options down to two. The first is to give up, acquiesce, simply lie down and surrender to the will of Washington and the administration of this president. I would not have asked any of you to work with me as a member of this very select group if I thought any of you would actually choose this option. For that, I am very proud of each of you for your will and determination. And now to the second option which I have reluctantly and prayerfully accepted in my own heart as the most appropriate course of action which I, as governor of the great state of Texas, should take."

Everyone sat still; the room remained deadly quiet...only shallow breathing broke the still silence. Simmons continued, now in a hushed coarse voice. "What I am going to share with you must be kept secret among each of you. Della has ruled that as governor, I am entitled to hold each of you to such secrecy. If there is anyone here who has a problem with this, they have my permission to leave this group— now!"

A few shifted in their seats and looked around at the others; no one left the room. The governor seemingly pleased, continued. "The term *secession*, to my knowledge has not been officially uttered openly in Texas since the civil war; yet today my friends, if I am judging each of you correctly over these several meeting sessions, I sense an extraordinary awareness, even commitment to do what has now become necessary. We are at a critical juncture within the country and our state, in particular, and in order to protect the people of Texas from unwanted and arduous acts being forced upon us, I am convinced we must take unprecedented actions. Della in her opinion as attorney general of Texas believes that we have a 'right,' if not lawful consent, to secede based on the early chapters of our Texas constitution. In short folks, there is an old Texas axiom, *'if your horse stumbles and falls, it's time to get out of the saddle'*. Della, would you elaborate on the finding you alluded to?"

Della needed little prompting. "Yes sir," she responded trying not to appear too eager. "The governor has mentioned that he asked that

I research our options including every 'loop hole' to determine if it is within any laws for Texas to extract itself from the United States." She cleared her throat and took in a deep breath. "If I may, Governor, let me say it and get it out on the table, The only viable option we have is that Texas must secede from the United States!"

She didn't pause for reaction and continued. "First, as I stated previously, there is no 'visible' provision either in the U.S. or Texas constitution that reserves the right for any state to secede from the union. However, the 'gem' I mentioned may lie within the constitution of the state of Texas which cites, *'Texas is a free and independent State, subject only to the Constitution of the United States.'* Let me state again that neither the Texas constitution, nor the Constitution of the United States, explicitly or implicitly disallows the secession of Texas from the United States. No doubt many legal scholars will argue differently. However, Texas joined the union voluntarily and I believe some scholars will vehemently argue that voluntary withdrawal could also be a lawful and viable option."

Della was suddenly interrupted by the vibrations of her pager, "I'm sorry, Governor, I had better take this. I still have an office to run, excuse me," she said and hurriedly went to the far corner of the meeting room.

Simmons acknowledged Della's interruption and without waiting for a response or questions, spoke. "I share Della's findings and her comments on our situation; if you recall, the president during his campaign told a national audience, *'We are getting very close to the time we can fundamentally transform the United States of America.'* Since his election over two years ago, he has provided us sufficient evidence that *'fundamentally'* he is living up to his word. The actions by this president and his administration which we are witnessing, the assessment previously shared with me by Della and what I believe she has reinforced today provides me with sufficient historical data to make the critical decision which I have. I recognize there are many preliminaries and much work to be done to carry out this act. But before I go farther, I would like to ask each of you for your reaction to these conclusions. I ask that you speak freely and share with me and your colleagues your feelings regarding whether you believe I am completely crazy or is secession viable? I will begin with you, Manny."

Caught by surprise, the speaker of the house suddenly found himself in the spotlight; he would have preferred to be elsewhere at the moment. He quickly sat upright, paused for a moment and spoke. "Yes, Governor, thank you," he replied, shifting around in his chair to address the group. "As you have stated, this is a bold move; bold indeed, more like insurrection, if you will forgive me. I can't disagree with any of Della's or the governor's assessments and his decision to free Texans from the tyranny of this perverse governing administration. To briefly recap my own reasoning for supporting you governor, last fall we completed a special session of the Texas legislature, the purpose of which was to address among other lesser issues, the immigration problem impacting our state. Our group here had noted that the immigration issue alone is already a major and growing problem affecting our Texas school systems, medical services and local economies. You are all aware of my heritage and I have a strong affinity for my birthright and that of my parents and relatives. But, I hasten to add, I am a Texan first, last and always. My parents immigrated legally into Texas and they claim our state as theirs. I also have great empathy for those clamoring to cross over the river and to live the lives we are so blessed to enjoy here in Texas. I will limit my remarks for now except to remind us that with our great affluence in America and within Texas especially, the unfettered freedoms which we mostly take for granted and boundless individual opportunities, we also create both envy and enemies alike. There are virtually millions clamoring to enter the United States, many of those just across the Rio Grande, to seek the land of opportunity. On the other side of the ledger there are an equal, if not an even greater number who want to kill us and destroy America. If the federal government fails to take action to create a strong national defense and security systems then we in Texas must make the right decisions to address both of these threats to our very being. My recent private thoughts have lead me to believe the choice to secede is our only one and will send a strong message not only to Washington, but to the entire country, that we will not be trod upon. I firmly support you, Governor. Lastly, when the time comes, I will ask Alex Mason to join me in contacting and working with each of our legislators whom I trust most personally to bring them into the plan and enlist their support."

"Thank you, Manny. Alex, what say you?" Simmons continued.

Alex Mason nodded politely. "Thank you, Governor, for the opportunity to be part of this august group of colleagues whom I have grown daily to respect. Sir, I will be honest with you, I was quite dubious about what I heard when I first joined this gathering. Now we are at a critical point and my first thought in response to your proposed decision is taking such a course as secession is very dangerous; it can bring the downfall of a nation. We witnessed that one hundred and fifty years ago with the civil war and God's hand mercifully guided us back to a unified nation, but not without the greatest blood bath in American history. I believe there may be the same potential with a decision to secede. But sir, Manny and I have privately discussed this possibility between ourselves and I also see no other choice that we have and, yes, you have my undivided support to proceed as you have suggested. Let me quickly add, this is must be carefully and comprehensively planned and carried out. Otherwise, we will fail and become the shame of the country, the world, and especially Texas will not have gained anything, only to have lost our stature for centuries to come. Thank you, sir."

"Thank you, Alex," Simmons replied. "I appreciate your candor and support. Reflecting a bit more on our rationale, I am sure all of you saw or heard about the recent cover of NEWSWEEK declaring, '*WE are all socialists now!*' When *that* magazine makes such a declaration, what does that tell us? Gordon, how about you?"

"Yes, sir," Gordon Giles nodded with a smile. "Governor, again permit me to thank you for including this old oil patch hand to join this extraordinary group of dedicated patriots. I have already commented on about all I can at this point, so count me on your team, governor, and tell me what you want me to do."

"Thanks, Gordon, I knew that I could depend on you," Simmons smiled. "You know", again trying to provide further commentary and justification for his decision, "another evolving threat to our freedoms which I haven't heard commented on yet is the so-called 'Fairness Doctrine' which will impose ever-increasing FCC regulations so severe that they will choke the conservative voices of talk radio. I thought I would just add that bit of insidious trash this so-called 'change' administration is working on. Okay, Lt. Governor Stauffer, Dan would you care to share your thoughts with us?"

Dan Stauffer had been sitting quietly listening and contemplating what he had heard during this controversial session; neither had he engaged in conversation on the issue with any of the members. He seemed reluctant to respond, but he knew that he must. He inhaled deeply and began to speak. "Governor, ladies and gentlemen, I must confess this has come so fast that I am having considerable difficulty absorbing the impact of it all. That doesn't let me off the hook; I am fully cognizant of the changes that this president and his congressional supporters are imposing on us. I, however, seriously wonder if attempting a form of anarchy, and that is precisely what an attempt at secession amounts to, is our only answer. Secondly, in my heart of hearts, I am convinced it will not work. It cannot work. I know a little constitutional law and specifically, *'Texas is a free and independent state, subject only to the Constitution of the United States.'* That's it pure and simple... Texas *'belongs'* to the United States of America and subject to all of its laws. Accordingly, if we pursue secession, or even the hint thereof, we will have the wrath of the entire federal government including law enforcement agencies, military forces, you name it, down on us. Each of us in this room will likely be charged with treason, particularly by this administration, and end up in prison. In the end, it will be our great state and its citizens that wind up at the brunt of every coldhearted means of retribution that can be meted out."

The lieutenant governor paused, sighed and continued. "Governor, this is not what you expected from me and I regret that I cannot share your feelings or your belief in the direction you wish to take Texas. With due respect for you, your office, all of you in this room and more importantly, Texas, at this point I will have to remain neutral in this action. For each of you if your truly wish to support the governor and his decision, please do not be influenced by my remarks or my position. Governor, I'm truly sorry and I sincerely wish you and Texas God's blessings." Dan Stauffer leaned back in his chair, dropped his head and placed his face in his hands.

The room was dead quiet; no one moved. Governor Simmons remained seated, rubbed his hands together slowly, his expression fixed in a blank stare. Finally he spoke. "Thank you, Dan; there is no substitute for candor. I appreciate your position and can only hope that as you further consider our situation and the option we must take you may reflect differently. The fact is, Dan, the nation has slipped so deeply into government intervention so affecting the lives of its citizens that most constitutional considerations have already been swept aside. The federal government is running roughshod over virtually every right guaranteed us by the constitution. Nationalization is the name of the game and with that comes pure socialism; history is our best teacher and replete with examples of failure. I sometimes wonder if the U.S. Constitution still holds true to the wishes and meanings as intended by the founding fathers. It seems to me that it has been diluted so much that we now have a free-for-all interpretation, and especially so by this president, his team, and the newer members of the Supreme Court. Maybe we should not use it for our guidance when facing what is now coming at us from Washington. Okay, enough of my rant; Zach, you have the largest responsibility in this state of maintaining law and order; where do you stand on our situation?"

The director of public safety pursed his lips, smiled and responded. "Well stated, Governor. I am not a bureaucrat so I will approach this situation from my position as a law enforcement officer; I was charged by late Governor Shahan to take over the state law enforcement agencies and to protect our people and property. If I interpret this new national trend properly, I foresee our country to soon be overshadowed by a federal police with the U.S. Constitution in shambles. That has been the historical approach taken by every socialist country in the world. They rely upon *Big Brother* and severe police tactics to keep the populace in check. You have alluded to failed examples including the former Soviet Union, Cuba, North Korea, Venezuela, to name some of the more obvious, past and present—and by all means not to overlook parts of Asia and the Middle East. This may sound like a scare tactic, but folks, I see it coming. Governor, I am with you and we need to move to declare our independence before it is too late. Thank you, sir, for your courage and determination."

"Thank you, Zach," Simmons nodded soberly. "You have nailed several critical parts of the perceived threat. Okay, General Lawhorn, may we have your thoughts?"

"Thank you, Governor, in short, full speed ahead!" Tom Lawhorn quickly responded. "I have listened carefully to each of our colleagues here, coupled with my own serious underlying fear of the Washington arena. With considerable reference to Lt. Governor Stauffer's position, this insidious decline in American values and taking away our independence has no apparent bottom." Looking directly at Dan Stauffer, he continued. "How much longer can we count on the U.S. Constitution as a defender of our basic human and individual rights? Our rights to define what constitutes a family; our belief in God; our right not to have an over-powering government looking down our throats; our right to uphold our own traditions, our values, our culture. This administration is and will continue to challenge the constitution right and left and with the appointment of liberal supreme court judges, they have the power to legitimize their 'changes.' It is hard for me to believe that with all the present and anticipated changes coming that this is the same constitution that I spent 30 years defending as a military officer. Hell no! I don't think so! I have some doubt as to whether one can seriously continue citing or referring to the U.S. Constitution as reasons why we should not exercise our legal option to secede. Again, with due respect for opposing opinions, our act to secede is much more legitimate and less anarchical than what this administration is doing with their radical changes. I will be able to comment further as we progress, Governor, thank you."

"Thank you, General," Simmons nodded. "I know where your heart and patriotism lie. We're in for a *helluva* fight, no doubt about it. General Mitchell, your comments?"

"Yes, Governor, thank you," Chris Mitchell replied. "Folks, as you know, while I have worn the uniform of the United States Air Force for more than thirty years, my roots have always remained deeply imbedded in Texas. That may sound a little hokey and pretentious in view of the fact that my oath of allegiance is to the United States of America, and of course it still is. But the evolving, eroding if you will, events of this administration is creating a dark cloud of doubt, anguish and even fear for many within our great state causing me to rethink my feelings and even my allegiance. Those are harsh words, perhaps even violating the Uniform Code of Military Justice, coming from a retired United States military officer. But after witnessing out and out poor leadership by our political leaders, I have reached the breaking point. I can no longer keep my frustration bottled up and I now find myself in a very awkward position; my honor rises above those who seek to destroy that for which I have lived and served. I fear, to use Manny's term, and it is fear, that the direction that Washington is taking the country will eventually bring us down to third world status or even lower, if that is possible. National security is undoubtedly being sacrificed for more social and domestic programs. Okay, so what can we do? What must we do to send a strong signal to Washington and to the nation that we will not sit by and be subjugated to a virtual slave state following their dictates? Since our two previous meetings, I thought about the option that the governor has chosen, including the potential consequences, and will say to you forthrightly here and now when basic rights of people are violated and or taken away, is it anarchy if one just says no? I say hell no, and I now believe that secession is our only option.

He paused briefly and continued, "Governor, you have made the only just and reasonable decision that is open for us to protect those values that many who have served in uniform defending this country to uphold. Now we must think only of Texas and believe that our decision to secede will be the right one. You can count me in to fully support you. Thank you, sir."

"Thank you, Chris," Simmons smiled. "May Pat Shahan rest in peace as his passing has brought together a circle of loyal Texans and new found friends; we would have likely not ever come to this point in time with this particular gathering. Not that Governor Shahan didn't have the same concerns and fears as we, but the opportunity to have fellow Texans and military officers assigned to senior positions join us in these serious discussions would be unlikely. These are many blessings in disguise. Okay, let's take a quick breather while the attorney general completes her business and we will then continue."

Chapter Eight

D ella Murphy quietly rejoined the group as they stood around in small talk.

"Ah, Della, you're back," the governor intervened, "would you continue and wrap up the discussion for us."

"Thank you, Governor," she acknowledged. "I apologize for the interruption." She then turned to face the group before her. "You have all heard my views and concerns and most, I believe, coincide with many of yours. First and most important, I fully support Governor Simmons in this difficult decision. I have been with him in private discussions and in these meetings and I can personally share with you that he has agonized greatly with the situation—the pros and cons—finally concluding that we have but one choice if we are to have any hopes of saving and preserving our Texas. So permit me to review, or perhaps further enlighten ourselves about the great largess we have within our state which is ours to both protect and to sustain us as we contemplate our decision to secede."

"First, Gordon Giles has shared with us his experience in the oil and gas industry which has been his life and is the life blood of Texas. We can literally supply all of the oil products that our state will need for the next 300 years. And, we can hope that during that protracted period, somebody may come up with alternative energy sources! (several chuckled at her snide remark). From our oil extraction, we refine and provide 85% of the gasoline requirements for the entire United States. Then there are our natural gas resources; we have all Texas will ever need for the rest of the foreseeable future.

"Generals Mitchell and Lawhorn are more aware than any of us; we have over 50% of the U.S. defense industry in Texas. If someone dared to invade us we have the Texas National Guard and Air Guard as well as our military reserves. Several of our military bases also have silos containing a nuclear arsenal which, if it ever becomes necessary, can serve as a countervailing power to *any nation* that threatens us. Along with all of that might, we have our state troopers and Texas rangers. This gives the *'Don't Mess With Texas'* watchword a whole new meaning!" Several snickered at her quip.

"And, what about the computer industry; we lead the nation in producing computer systems, parts, chips and communications— Dell, EDS, Raytheon, Texas Instruments, INTEL, NORTEL, and Motorola— the list goes on and those are the *national* 'biggies.' There are hundreds of other smaller technology industries that feed the larger ones and the nation. That leads us to the space industry; NASA is right here in Texas. You might say we control space!"

Della was on a roll as she confidently laid out her thoughts. "With trade, Texas has three of the largest ports in the United States. Three of the ten largest cities in the U.S. are in Texas.

"What about health and medical care? We possess the largest and most comprehensive medical research, treatment and trauma centers in the world, cancer research, burn trauma and treatment, and long-term care. The Houston medical complex alone has over 65,000 employees. Education! We have more colleges, universities and institutions of higher learning than any other state in the union. You know what and who they are; The University of Texas, *'Hook 'em Horns!'* Rice, *'Yea,* Owls!' Texas A&M, *'Gig 'em!'* Texas Tech, *'Go Raiders!'* Baylor, SMU, UNT, TWU--hope I didn't short anyone in this room—there are hundreds of others equally important to the education and research foundations in Texas. You might say ivy grows better in Texas!"

She continued. "Speaking of food; I don't know anybody but Yankees who would eat ivy. Texas is totally self-sufficient in food production— beef, poultry, swine as well as virtually every variety of grain, fruit and vegetables. The Gulf of Mexico provides more seafood varieties than about anywhere in the world and in abundance. Can we expand our production facilities and crop output? We have more tillable land in Texas than California, New York, New Jersey, Connecticut, Delaware, Hawaii, Massachusetts, Rhode Island and Vermont combined. If measured against the economies and populations of all nations, Texas would rank 39th. Those are the facts, my friends. Are we capable of becoming independent? We ARE independent!

"Now, let me briefly return to some of the legal issues to help alleviate any remaining doubts about our selected option. Lt. Governor Stauffer has alluded to anarchy should we declare our independence and that could be a serious concern. Most of this we have already been over, but there is a quirk in the history and international law that for the most part has been officially ignored. This may shock you, but this finding is in direct contrast to what we might have been led to believe. But, it's clear. The people of Texas were tricked into adopting the U.S. Constitution back on December 29th, 1845. The fraudulent actions of the 10th Congress of the United States with the passage of a constitutional amendment to annex Texas was done in order to facilitate the invasion of Mexico and gain seaports in Mexico and California. The quirk or twist of fate is that the constitutional amendment, including the Annexation Resolution to absorb Texas, was never ratified by the separate states as was and is the law. This legally means that due to this lack of ratification, one can say that Texas never officially joined the Union. The documentation, or lack thereof, is clear and supports Texas as continuing to be a legitimate, lawful, sovereign and independent nation. Governor, my fellow Texans, because and due to the circumstances that now confront us, I believe we have a legal basis for our decision and it is time for us to take Texas back!"

"Thank you, Della, for the extraordinary research findings!" Governor Simmons hurriedly replied; applauding as Della completed her comments. It seems that I can now conclude a *near* unanimous collective decision to move forward. We have much work to do and little time within which to do it. I am sure your minds are buzzing with questions, apprehension and excitement, all bundled up together. So, rather than enter into lengthy dialogue, let's close this session for now, return to our separate ways and reflect on what we have before us. I hope to contact each of you in a day or so and schedule an action-planning meeting. I am hopeful that you, Chris and Tom, can stick around Austin for just a few more days.

"Gene, I will need you to assist me in developing a draft schedule. Therein we will need to assign responsibilities to our various members, recruit additional trusted members for special expertise and support. We need to get an agenda together as quickly as possible. I want to begin putting the decision in motion with a detailed plan. I want to thank each of you; well done! Oh, Chris, Tom and Zach, can I visit with you for a moment?"

As the members gathered themselves to leave the meeting, a confident but measured grin eased across the lips of the governor who was now convinced that the forthcoming days would take them in an unprecedented, but necessary tenuous direction. Except for Lt. Governor Stauffer, each member of the group outwardly appeared to reflect a sense of exhilaration perhaps coupled with apprehension as the reality of the drama settled upon them. As Texans, they were fully aware that the direction the governor had openly asserted was historical, indeed radical. But as Della had confirmed, secession can be considered a historical and inherent right of the people of Texas. Each appeared to take comfort in feeling that the decision to secede had the support of one another. Most also believed that Texans across the state would support their decision The only exception in his group was the lieutenant governor. Simmons would have to deal with him in the coming days.

Dan Stauffer darted for the exit without saying a word. As the remaining members rose from their chairs and as if on cue stood in place for a moment, eyed one another and then automatically formed a circle around the coffee table. Reaching across, they each clasped the hand of the other. Attorney General Murphy began to whisper a barely audible prayer.

"Our Father in Heaven, these are difficult times for our people and the integrity of our great state of Texas and nation. We pray that this journey that we are about to undertake is the right direction for all the right reasons. We ask Your blessings on these brave men as they commit themselves for the good of all men. Lead, guide and direct us individually and collectively that we may make the right and proper decisions for the benefit of all Texans. God bless Texas. In His Holy name, Amen."

All but the governor, Mitchell, Lawhorn and Hollis left the room. "Oh, Della, Gene," Simmons summoned. "You two can also stay."

They all remained standing. "Della thank you for those beautiful words; so very appropriate as this time, thank you. Okay, what I want to do initially is develop a preliminary action plan, execution plan, if you will," the governor began. "Chris, you and Tom are the experts in this area. We need a plan to seal off our state once we make our declaration known; the borders in particular. We will also need to set up 'entry stations' at all major and in some cases, minor highway locations from New Mexico, Arkansas, Oklahoma and Louisiana. I am getting ahead of myself of course, that sort of work should be left to Zach here. He owns the state troopers and rangers. So your plan will need to be comprehensive, coordinated between different agency heads, troopers, rangers, and I presume we can count on the Texas national guard, can we not, Tom? I know, as governor, that I will have to activate the guard. I will do that at the appropriate time as called for in the plan. What else? Zach, as we get closer to S-Day and more and more people join us creating more possibilities of a 'leak', I would like for your troopers to keep a watchful eye on all of our families, just in case. Okay, now which of you wants to step forward to be the head honcho—overall coordinator—to pull it all together and report directly to me?"

Tom Lawhorn spoke up, "I recommend Chris, Governor. I will be pretty busy with the guard units and Zach will be equally busy with his people."

"What do you think, Chris?" Simmons asked.

"Sure, Governor," Mitchell responded. "These two are also experts; I will be pleased to work with them and between the three of us, we'll get it together for you. Let me raise a serious issue. We have several large military installations in the state; the commanders are active duty military officers and when this comes down, they are going to take orders from the Pentagon. I am not asking for guidance; I just want to raise the point between us at the outset. We'll get back to you, but it's one that will require some considerable strategy."

"Good point, Chris," Simmons frowned. "You guys work it and let me know your thoughts. Okay, it has been a long day; we're all in overload, so let's close it out for now. Della, you motioned to visit with me?"

"Yes, sir," she replied, "for just a few minutes."

The others departed and after the door was closed, Della began. "Governor, the pager message I received was a call from an attorney friend of mine and he told me that a group calling themselves the '*Texas Advocacy Coalition*', or TAC, as they're calling it. They're getting organized in Houston with ties in the DFW area, San Antonio, Lubbock,

Amarillo and El Paso. Their agenda is not unlike ours here and you will be familiar with the names of the two leaders heading the group, George Comstock and Bill Clark."

"Hmmmm," Simmons nodded.

"According to my source," Della continued. "They have already pulled together a dozen or more prominent active players from Houston and Dallas with others coming on board from across the state. I thought you would find this interesting."

"You mean they are addressing the same concerns that we are; along the same lines?" Simmons quickly asked. "You're telling me that they are likewise frightened with this administration's moves toward socializing our country, liberalizing immigration, gay rights, and so on?"

"Yes, sir, that's what he says it appears to be," she replied. "He was invited to join a meeting last night in Houston and listened to their agenda outline. Of course, he doesn't know that we have been in discussions on virtually the same issues. He called me because of my position as AG and thought I should know that such *seditious* unrest and activities are taking place. I asked him if there was a militant flavor to their discussions and he said absolutely not, the group of six or seven in the session he attended are all professional men and women; attorneys, academics and businessmen. They did require him to sign a pledge of confidentiality and invited him to join them in future discussions. Interesting, huh?"

Simmons smiled, "So we are not alone in our concerns with the growing threat, are we? Della, I am very interested in this 'advocacy coalition' group. Do you feel comfortable contacting Comstock or Clark, either direct or through your friend? I recognize the sensitivity and don't want to frighten them off. What do you think?"

"I need to think about it, Governor," she replied, the proposition running through her thoughts. "I don't want to compromise my contact; let me think about how I might go about it."

"Okay, fine," Simmons replied, nodding. "I understand; keep me posted. Well, let's continue on here and you and I can get back to this later...very interesting; thanks, Della."

As the governor and Della departed the building walking to their cars, Gordon Giles rushed over to them with an apparent sense of revelation on his face. "Governor, Oh, I forgot to mention in all the excitement today that I had a call last week from a banker friend of mine there in Houston; I think you may know him, George Comstock. George invited me to a meeting with a few friends, he said, to discuss what seems to me to be about the same dilemma we are about here today."

Governor Simmons made eye contact with Della with a wink and smile. She immediately thought to herself; "This is our connection with the 'TAC'."

Giles went on to say, "I couldn't make his meeting but if you would like I will stay in close contact with him."

The governor patted him on the back. "That would be great, Gordon, and perhaps at some point we can get back together for a chat."

"Will do, Governor, See 'ya." They shook hands and Giles went on his way.

The following morning Governor Simmons called Gene Todd and asked him to set up the next meeting for the coming weekend at the same Lakeway hotel if possible and indicated that it is vital to have all members in attendance. He suggested that the meeting start at 9:00 a.m. Saturday. The governor then went about performing his regular duties, reflecting no indication to his staff or others that the major event of which he was taking full responsibility was unfolding.

Gene Todd contacted Della Murphy and Jacque assisted him in coordinating the meeting with the team members. They understood the travel procedures and hotel arrangements; each appeared eager to get on with the business of establishing a detailed plan.

Meanwhile, Chris Mitchell, Tom Lawhorn and Zach Hollis spent two fast days developing a draft plan to present to the governor. In addressing the issue of military installations in Texas, Mitchell suggested that they concern themselves with major facilities, Ft. Hood, Ft. Bliss, Dyess Air Force Base, Sheppard Air Force Base, Naval Air Stations at Ft. Worth and Corpus Christi. Their plan would include Chris visiting the commanders of Dyess, Sheppard and NAS Ft. Worth; Tom would visit the commanders of Ft. Bliss, Ft. Hood and Corpus Christi. Their approach would be one of being a representative of the governor's homeland security task force. Their respective military ranks would provide them credibility with the installation commanders and assist them in advising that they were conducting a highly confidential survey of the facilities, the unit mission, number of personnel on base, etc. Since this was a state of Texas program, they would request that the commanders keep it confidential from within and to not elevate it up the chain. They would also be briefed that a soon-to-be security exercise would be conducted by the Texas National Guard and reserve forces and they would be notified a day or so before. A list of contacts of the senior officers to be notified would be recorded containing telephone numbers and email addresses. No action would be required of the respective military units; only that either state troopers or Texas rangers would show up at their main gates, work with the military security personnel and "monitor" activities. They still needed to work out contingency plans in the event "something went wrong."

Zach Hollis agreed with the military installation approach plan and would also develop domestic plans to include bringing county law enforcement agencies along the major highway entry routes from the border states into a state security network to monitor and control access into Texas when instructed to do so. The governor would activate the Texas National Guard and reserves two days before S-Day. Tom Lawhorn would coordinate the national guard to merge some guard troops with the Border Patrol along the Mexican border, including El Paso and other principal entry points. He was confident that the border patrol agents would readily cooperate since they were "all" Texans to begin with.

Zach Hollis raised an issue he said that somewhat troubled him and that was the FBI. "They report directly to Washington," he said. "They are extremely independent and bureaucratic and I doubt that few of them are Texans or hold any particular allegiance to Texas. My advice is that we let them be; they have a Special Agent in Charge or S.A.C., in every one of our major cities. I know most of the respective SAC's and speak to them frequently on cases of interest. But again, they are independent and internally protective. So, again, for now I suggest we let them be." Tom and Chris agreed.

The overall plan would of necessity be flexible and subject to unforeseen shifts and changes depending on the circumstances. They agreed networking with all the agencies involved would be critically sensitive. No one could predict individual or local reactions when the governor's declaration became known.

To avoid unusual attention to herself and her AG position, Della Murphy sent Jacque Adams to Houston to meet Gordon Giles whom she had coordinated with to contact the TAC leaders there. Jacque would be unknown to the group and she initially introduced herself as a very patriotic Texan with serious interests in preserving Texas' integrity and independence. Based on Giles's endorsement, she was welcomed by George Comstock and Bill Clark as they were very interested in expanding their cause and getting more patriots to join. After several hours of discussion, exchange of ideas, strategies, etc, Jacque revealed that she was a direct representative of the governor and shared the secession plan with them. Comstock and Clark were elated and agreed to keep it under their hats until the governor was ready to publically announce.

Jacque assisted them in developing a formal TAC support plan. George Comstock would become the senior TAC leader and Bill Clark, the CEO. Comstock was invited to come to Austin and attend the forthcoming meeting while Clark would personally travel to each of the TAC centers around the state assisting them in formally organizing their cells and recruiting trusted members and expanding the units into representative numbers. Jacque and Comstock developed an action plan which included a communications network to bring all of the cells into a central reporting link in Houston. On S-Day, this central unit would become fully operational. Caution and discipline were the watchwords and especially in using the 'secession' word. She warned that confidentiality was mandatory—a single "leak" and the secession plan would be compromised and likely killed. And, "no *wanna be's*, or self-styled mavericks," she said. "The governor is our leader and the chain of command emanates from him only, including all directives; coordination and cooperation are imperative!"

Chapter Nine

The week passed quickly; on Saturday morning, Zach Hollis met the governor for the drive to Lakeway. En route, Hollis briefed the governor on the joint plan that he, Mitchell and Lawhorn had developed. Simmons was very pleased. They arrived in time to greet the other team members, have a sweet roll and coffee. Della introduced Gordon Comstock to the governor and the other members. After pleasantries, Simmons announced over the chatter, "Ladies and gentlemen shall we gather in the meeting room and get started?"

Once everyone was seated, Governor Simmons positioned himself where he could see everyone without having to shift around. "First off, thank you all for working your schedules so you could attend this critically important meeting," he began. "Secondly, I want to officially welcome our new member, George Comstock. George represents a very large and an extremely important wing of our task force. I will ask him later to describe his role and mission. Folks, at our last meeting and especially this gathering under my leadership I again remind you that in Washington these meetings would only be construed as acts of treason, pure and simple. I am willing to accept that premise and I must presume by the continued presence of each of you, based upon what you know from our previous gatherings, you also understand and accept that assertion. Am I correct?"

There were a few audible "yeses" with all but Dan Stauffer nodding in the affirmative. He remained quiet, his face pallid. Governor Simmons had all but ignored him following the last meeting. They had bumped into one another several times during the week and remained formally cordial, although it was painfully apparent that there were strained feelings between the two. Simmons rationalized, "Stauffer is a brilliant and thoughtful individual, and he will have to work this out in his own mind. No matter what, I do not think he will let the cat out of the bag."

⌒

The 'strained' feelings were far deeper than Governor Simmons could possibly have fathomed. In order to get a better feel of where Dan was headed, Della Murphy asked Jacque Adams to contact the lieutenant governor shortly after the previous meeting and they met twice to discuss the unfolding secession drama, each with a differing agenda. It was clear that Stauffer's feelings were not far from being intellectually and sympathetically aligned with the President of the United States. He shared with Jacque that he felt a kinship with the brilliant and youthful president, and his far-reaching ideas for America.

"I don't share the perceived onerous impositions on Texas that Simmons or the others feel," he said. "I sincerely believe that the president is looking far beyond the horizon, more so than any president ever has. He is seeking parity for America with other nations; he desperately wants peace for all mankind and with all nations, a world community, if you will. And, in order to get there, we must jointly sacrifice and share in all resources."

Jacque Adams did not subscribe entirely to Stauffer's philosophy, but understood and grasped much of it. Her agenda was much more personal and she had been waiting for an opportunity to share it. She told Stauffer that while listening to Simmons' speeches and appeal to the group over the past few months she now believed him to be weak, not intellectually bright, more of a *'cowboy'* and one looking for short-term notoriety without looking very far ahead into the future.

"He has no idea or a clue regarding the consequences of secession should he go through with it," she smirked. "The feds will come down on us like a runaway freight car and wipe out every one of us who gets caught in front of it. I may have been with him in the beginning, but the more I heard from him and his group I knew they were headed in a direction that would lead to a calamity and I would be caught in it. Dan, I now believe we need to consider another strategy that gives us more power and control over the eventual fiasco that awaits Simmons."

During their second late night meeting, she made her move. "Dan, here's my proposal," she began coyly. "If you will join me in supporting this façade; by that, go through the motions of supporting Simmons' secession attempt and if it is quasi-successful, then we will declare our own coup. Between the two of us, and with the support from many others, who I am convinced they don't want to go in this direction, we can then take charge of the leadership of Texas."

She smiled and continued. "Within his little task force, there are one or two who I believe I can count on." She waited for a reaction; he didn't respond. "Dan," she continued confidently. "If he proceeds with his secession plan, and I am convinced he is going to, and if you will support me, as soon as he makes his declaration by working with Washington, in particularly the president's staff and the U.S. Attorney General, I will bring unbearable forces on him and Della Murphy. As the feds move in to restore order, I would hope to be named to replace her as attorney general and you as governor. If that didn't happen immediately, then I would seek immediate impeachment of Simmons. As the new governor you could then take charge of Texas, contact the president and request amnesty for all Texans except those directly involved in the secession scheme. As your attorney general, I will file charges for treason against Simmons and the rest of his followers. And in the end, you and I can have this state all to ourselves."

"We avoid the secession tumult that you have revulsion for and as AG, I can be recognized as more than just being a young female stuck in an administrative pocket."

Stauffer studied Jacque coyly; he did not need to respond. He was not surprised by her provocative notion; he had heard that she was exceedingly ambitious, not unlike himself, and was one tough calculating young lady. He waited for her to provide more details...

"Good," Simmons continued with his remarks. "For the benefit of George, let me again provide a quick summary of where I believe we are and why we intend to take a very difficult but necessary action. The United States is in increasing turmoil and the last national election serves to confirm that the majority of voters—outside of most Texans and a few within other southern states—are in favor or shifting toward a socialist and extreme liberal form of government that is less concerned with national security than they are with promoting multiple forms of diversity and unacceptable social programs. That was confirmed by the overwhelming election results coming mostly from liberal states. Much potential taxing legislation and new financial regulations are being passed in each congressional session along with the past bailouts of banks, financial loan institutions and the automobile industry. Thus far within this economic downturn being experienced across the country, Texas has managed to hold its own, but the reality is that we will also soon be consumed by the same affliction that is being suffered by California, the upper Midwestern states and the Northeast. Other states are experiencing high debts, double digit unemployment, and home foreclosure rates are skyrocketing. Before too long, the federal government will begin looking to the more prosperous of us to help bail out those who have bankrupted themselves. I believe that is inevitable."

"Let me now call on my friend, George Comstock, the newest member of our '*rebellious*' group, to give us a quick review of his work."

George Comstock rose from his seat confidently. "Thank you, Governor," he began; a big smile on his face. "My, my, never underestimate Texans! When Jacque made her subtle visit to Houston last week, I first thought to myself, '*here's Austin politics sticking their noses into our business again.*' Boy was I surprised! Bill Clark and I could not have been more pleased. For those of you who are not aware I will be very brief. Bill Clark, a close friend and banker in Houston and I, way back last summer, began to be fearful if not downright scared of what was coming out of Washington politics. So we began to contact mutual friends around the state, most of whom are professional and very influential, to share our concerns with them. Long story short, we quickly organized the Texas Advocacy Coalition, TAC, for short. We were overwhelmed and amazed when we discovered the serious discontent throughout the state, for all the reasons and concerns I understand you have been discussing for quite some time. With Jacque's assistance, we are in the process of formally organizing ourselves into a cohesive and structured operation.

When 'S-Day' arrives, we will be out in force throughout the state rallying around the governor's proclamation and reinforcing confidence wherever needed. We will not be a militant mob, but a unified patriotic group of Texans. Our maxim is peaceful and lawful support. As I speak, we are establishing a communications network and quietly expanding our partnership throughout the state. The good news in this respect is that we will promptly move to align ourselves with the TEA, 'tax enough already' Party group. As you know, they have already held well-attended meetings throughout Texas and several other states. In the past mid-term elections, TEA party candidates did very well.

"Governor, some time ago, you spoke to this group during a rally in San Antonio and you made some very interesting remarks that were well listened to by this group and, as you know, caught the eye of press. Many of these folks will also join us. Thank you, sir, for inviting me and we are ready when you are!"

"Well, what can I say?" Governor Simmons nodded with elation. "So, to bring it to a head with all of what's been said about the U.S. government and Texas we now have a choice, albeit desperate, it is a choice we can make ourselves. We can either sit here in our great state while gradually having our well-being erode from beneath us without resistance, or we can put into play what we have decided and that is to move to take dramatic measures that hopefully prevent a complete demise of every tradition we believe in. I don't have all the answers; neither do I believe that any one of us has, much less the consequences of the path I have guided you toward. So collectively, among this special and select group, I am hopeful that on this day we can fully accept the option that we have chosen and begin to finalize a more detailed plan to carry it out. If I believed there were viable alternatives, I would not hesitate to consider them. Without question, our decision and actions will be viewed by many as gloom and doom, bordering on insanity, that is why I value your judgment and candor which confirms our common concerns. For any one of you who opposes our thoughts, now is the time to opt out or say no and you may go on your way without any hindrance." No one moved to exit the meeting.

Governor Simmons took in a deep breath, exhaling slowly, "Okay, we have made the decision; now we move into the operational planning phase. I want to hear from each of you as to your anticipated role, suggested timing of the operation, possible contingencies and overall expectations.

"First let's hear from our military representatives. "General Mitchell, would you give us a quick overview of how your initial plans are coming along?"

"Thank you, Governor" Chris Mitchell replied. "General Lawhorn, Zach Hollis and I met this past week and I believe we have addressed several major parts of the plan to support the execution of your decision. I don't believe it necessary to take up the time of everyone to go into all of details here and now. Suffice to say, I believe we have the bases covered regarding calming the potential reaction of our federal military installations within the state as well as the civil factions. Zach has already shared that with you to some extent. In sum, I believe we collectively need to organize ourselves into planning and functioning groups with each focusing on what they can best contribute to the overall strategy and execution of the plan. We will follow your lead, Governor."

"Okay, great! Thank you, General," Simmons replied. "I do have some items that need to be considered and I will discuss those with you in a few minutes. On that note, General Lawhorn, will you share your thoughts with us?"

"Thank you, Governor," Tom Lawhorn replied. "Sir, I believe Chris has covered our planning quite well, so I will not elaborate further. We will be ready."

"Good, thank you, Tom," Simmons responded. "I have already heard privately from Zach and I am pleased with all the progress made in a short time this past week.

The other side of the 'secession coin', so to speak is 'what happens after?' We must recognize that once we make our move, the president and his administration will come down hard; how hard, we don't have any idea probably police action, prompt stopping of mail service, social security and federal retirement checks, to name a few. Are we prepared for the consequences? I know these are latter day questions, but I want to be open and upfront with all of you. Do any of you have any questions or trepidations along these lines?"

No one spoke at first, then Gordon Giles raised his hand. "Governor, we have made a decision to proceed. Yes, we may endure a few hardships for a short time, but if we come together as Texans should and will, we will make it over the bumps in the road. Making the decision is the hard part; carrying it out is the easier of the two."

A spurt of applause broke out in the room.

"Thank you, all of you!" Simmons said, smiling. "Okay, we need to get to the timing and work our schedule accordingly. As I mentioned, there are also several more planning elements that need to be considered and they include actions before and after our declaration of secession. One of these is that we must create a cabinet for the new Republic of Texas. I will assume at this point that I will serve as the president and Dan will take on the vice president position. I would plan on calling an election after the first year for new candidates who wish to challenge any of the leadership positions in the Republic. In that the position of secretary of defense is important, I would recommend that General Mitchell assume this role with Tom Lawhorn as his deputy. General Mitchell's last active duty day ended a few weeks ago and he is free to carry out his role without federal military legalities. I have already asked Chris to head up a task force comprising himself, Tom, and Zach to conduct an earlier review of the larger security concerns we would face before, during, and especially after S-Day. As he indicated, I believe he is ready for the challenge. Perhaps Della could be appointed secretary of state and Gordon, secretary of commerce. However, I will also ask Della for the present to also continue serving as attorney general for the new Republic until we have a degree of understanding and stability in how our new court and legal system will work. In your planning sessions, please recommend others to fill posts that I have not covered herein.

"Della has suggested and I concur, and believe all of you will as well, that is we initially retain the major portions of the U.S. Constitution and at a later time revisit each part for its relevance to our Republic. Along with this, our court system should essentially remain the same and soon after S-Day we will choose 10 judges from our State Superior Court to serve initially as the supreme court of the Republic. Della will get that process moving."

His thoughts were racing as he continued. "As each of you go through the phases of the planning process keep in mind that from day one we need to have a functioning government. This means not only having departments, but commissions along with rules to initially guide us through the first few months or so. We need to recognize that we are undertaking the establishment of a fully operating government including monetary and financial systems, tax codes, and education systems. Everything that the federal system provides for now must be adopted or modified to serve the purposes of the Republic of Texas. We all need to ponder these requirements in considerable depth.

"Regarding specific roles in your planning, Della, Chris, Tom and Gene have their tasks outlined, I would like for Manny and Alex to examine just how our new Republic's legislative bodies will function. I will need their recommendations regarding senior leadership positions once implemented. Promptly before our announcement, I would like Manny to contact the President of Mexico and other nearby Spanish speaking governments to advise them of our decision and that they should not attempt to make a move to disrupt our actions. We desire their cooperation and will seek to establish immediate trade relationships with each.

"Alex, as we approach the announcement window, I want you to contact our two U.S. senators and our representatives and request they return immediately to Texas for further guidance. In that our new Republic will be divided into five states, some of these legislators may very well represent those newly formed governments.

"Manny, Alex, as part of your contacting roles, have one of your trusted political friends, perhaps one of our U.S. senators, call the Secretary General of the United Nations as well as the Prime Ministers of Canada, Great Britain, the President of France and the Chancellor of Germany to advise them of our actions. Also assure them that we want friendly relations with each and highly desire them as trading and cultural exchange partners."

Simmons continued to issue instructions and requests from his well-planned and unscripted syllabus. "Manny, there is one other thing I would like to ask of you; immediately after the secession announcement, I would like for you to address the various Hispanic groups throughout the state to reassure them that they have nothing to fear from this change. Alex, I would like for you to do the same with other minority constituents and our religious leaders? From the start, we do not want to isolate any particular group."

"Will do!" replied Manny and Alex in unison.

Now, Gordon; in order to quell banking and financial fears, at the right moment you or one of your banker friends should contact the chairmen of the top 20 corporations and 10 largest financial institutions, including the Federal Reserve Board, to advise them that the Republic of Texas will continue to honor all business contracts, relationships and obligations. With all your ties within the petroleum and business industries, you would be the one to provide them the necessary assurances and confidence that we are making all the right decisions for the benefit of Texas."

"I would like to request each of our group to assist Gordon with his tasks in any way he wishes. For the time being, we will keep the U.S. dollar as our national currency. What have I left out? Oh, yes, perhaps we should also retain and use the U.S. Postal Service until we create our own system. Do any of you have difficulty or further suggestions with any of these?"

Gordon Giles and George Comstock each responded in the affirmative.

"Oh, Governor", Gordon interjected. "You mentioned that upon our seceding, the government would likely stop retirement checks, social security, military retirement and so forth. I have several of my retired employees, and a few of them are also military retirees, living in Canada, Mexico and parts of Europe, and they are receiving their monthly checks without issue. Legally though, I am not a lawyer, but most would say that it is their money; they were guaranteed these benefits. I would think that the U.S. would have no right to stop these benefit checks. At least that is my take on this issue."

"Gordon is probably right, Governor," Manny responded. "Only the test of time will tell."

"That could be a potentially serious issue," the governor acknowledged. "Hopefully it will not become one to concern us. Before we move to Zach Hollis' role, one hour before I make the secession announcement, I will personally call the President of the United States and inform him of our decision and respectfully request that he think carefully about any corrective action before the government acts precipitously. I will inform him that we will work closely with all U.S. military facilities located in Texas and over the next few days will allow those who wish to leave the state to do so. Further, I will assure him that we want to cooperate fully in working out a relationship with the other U.S. government facilities located within the Republic. Following General Mitchell's team recommendation, I will close my conversation with the president by advising him that I have activated all Texas National Guard and reserve forces and that we have essentially sealed off the major interstate and secondary highways leading into Texas from Oklahoma,

Louisiana, New Mexico and Arkansas. I hope he gets the picture that we are prepared to defend our new Republic.

"During the time I am in contact with the president, Dan, I would ask that you place a call to the governors of our border states advising them that we have taken the action to secede and we will transition toward a smooth flow of traffic and other exchanges within a few days if not sooner." The governor did not wait for Dan to respond.

"Returning to our individual assignments, I would like for Zach Hollis to act as the Republic's chief, internal security; he already has several good ideas regarding how to secure the new Republic.

"George, you and Bill Clark represent the banking industry and will play an important role in the success of our move to independence. If you agree, I would like for you to assist Gordon as he deals with the financial and potential monetary challenges that we will likely face. Also, I look forward to your continued development of your TAC and *TEA* groups as they prepare to activate gatherings, meetings, public and private, to voice the necessary strong support at the moment we will really need such. Hopefully you will have some good luck with getting the press to cover the events. No doubt there will be some liberal group who will react, especially from the Austin academics and maybe some from students here from other states."

"Generals Mitchell and Lawhorn along with Zach and I have discussed the potential for having to impose martial law, if and when it should become necessary. At this point none of us believe it will reach that level."

Simmons continued, "There will be numerous other details requiring our attention as we get closer to *The Day*. It's an all new experiment and we will no doubt encounter untold and unexpected surprises. To give all of you sufficient time to work your issues, I will schedule another meeting about 60 to 90 days from now; hopefully by then we will have many of the details in place. In your planning sessions, I want each of you to brain-storm all the possible contingencies we might encounter between now and the announcement—including what we might expect in the days afterward. You will need special assistance and support staff for your key positions; try to choose them carefully. Place special emphasis on 'need' and 'trust.' We must think smart and wisely always remembering why we have chosen this option. Okay, anything else from anyone?" No one responded.

Chapter Ten

Governor Simmons was ecstatic; jumping from one issue to the other. "Well," he finally said; "before we break, let me mention just one more important issue which hasn't surfaced to any degree in our deliberations and that is the news media. Who among you has an 'in' or contact with the media outlets, local or major, with newspapers, radio, Internet bloggers, TV? Gene, of course, is our PR '*hound*' and has contact with most of them throughout the state, but if any of you has a particular business or personal relationship with any of them, let Gene know and perhaps we can work up a '*pre-nuptial*' agreement.

"One reminder in that regard, Gene, immediately before and after S-Day, you will to be releasing news briefs to tell the world what we doing and why. If you need any additional special requirements or people to carry it all out, let me know."

"I believe we are in good shape, Governor; we'll be ready," Gene responded. "I would like to remind our group that any questions from the press, or anyone for that matter pops up, please refer it to me. As we get closer to the secession date and our plan gets more widely discussed, the more likely there will be a leak. I would like to have an agreement on a single response if someone is asked about what's going on. My suggestion is something along the line of, 'It's just someone spinning what the governor mentioned to the TEA group.' And on S-Day, of course, a much more comprehensive press release citing; 'because of the U.S. government's intrusion into the lives of ordinary Texans, in particular from this president's policies, we had no other choice but to declare our independence from the growing oppressiveness. The less said the better and let it evolve. If any questions arise concerning any of your planning functions, I will give you a heads up before I send the press to you for an answer. That's my suggestion, sir."

"Thank you, Gene, good points. General Mitchell and General Lawhorn, as well as Zach, have proposed that we establish a 24-7 Command Center inside the capitol building with direct communication links to the national guard and other security forces. I would also like video camera coverage of all potential trouble spots such as the highway blockades, military facilities, and our legislature offices fed directly into the Command Center. We will have beds, kitchens and bathrooms installed to support the operation; there will likely be times when several of us will need to be immediately available for emergency situations. I will have this set up under the guise of developing a 'Homeland Security Center.' It should be ready to go within a month. Prior to S-Day, I want each of you to spend some time at the Command Center to insure it has the tools or resources you require to carry out your particular duties and responsibilities. On the morning that I announce, each of you should be in the center. I plan to make my secession speech on the front steps of the capitol building. Following that, all other releases and communication will be delivered from the Command Center. Does everyone agree and are there any questions?"

"Good plan, Governor," Della quickly responded. "I will ask Jacque to keep an eye on the Command Center project and let you know when it's completed, tested, and ready for use."

Looking about the trusted members standing before him, he smiled. "While I have been doing most of the talking and riding a little high in the saddle, I apologize; I would like to wrap this up. Do any of you have any comments or reactions to what I have covered to this point? Have I left out anything?"

"Excellent assessment, Governor," Chris Mitchell responded. "You've outlined our goals and objectives, and I believe you are right on target."

"Ditto," replied Della, smiling.

"Thank you. One final question for now," he concluded, attempting to close all possible loopholes. "Are we all clear on our respective roles in the eventual execution of the mission?"

There were collective nods and 'yeses' by all but Dan, who was starring with a blank look on his face.

"Della, you are the overall planning coordinator. Over the next two months while waiting for our next meeting as you receive progress reports from the planning groups, I would like to review the details of the major components of the plan as they come in. Our next meeting should be the last before we execute the plan. We will set the date and time for a rehearsal and the execution. I am feeling more confident with each session with you folks and I have no doubt that we will be ready when the day arrives.

"Gene, you will assist me in developing my proclamation. In my remarks, I want to explain to the people of Texas what our vision is for the new Republic. Develop a draft and then we can go over it together. Okay, we are almost there; when do we take the big step? What is the preferred date and time of the proclamation?"

There was a shuffling of feet and looking around among the group. Della Murphy finally spoke. "March 2nd, Texas Independence Day, Governor!" she replied assertively.

Several applauded and someone else added, "That's a Tuesday; make your proclamation at five a.m., governor. That will catch the media and everybody else off guard."

General Mitchell interjected, "Perhaps we should consider a Saturday for the announcement; that's a slow media day and most military and government departments are in a stand-down mode. That would make it more difficult for any of them to quickly respond. Sunday, too, is generally a quiet day"

"That's a good thought, Chris," Tom Lawhorn quickly responded. "That reminds me, it would be ideal if we had a way to quietly get the word out to all Texans serving in the U.S. military that they will have the option of returning to Texas and become part of our defense force. I'll admit that would be a tall order and no doubt compromise our plans, so I'll drop that one. Chris and I know most of the generals and admirals in the defense department and I suggest at the right moment we should inform them of what is about to take place."

"That may be a good idea, Tom," Chris responded, "but I believe it may also be a tall, if not impossible, task to get to all of those guys in a coordinated manner. But of equal importance, it is the lack of a confidential way to do it without one or several of them blowing our cover. I suggest what we might do is to make informal contact with a few select senior officers whom we can trust to sit tight until the announcement; even then, there is a risk of compromise."

"I agree," Tom acknowledged. "Perhaps you and I can work out a plan to make a few confidential contacts."

George Comstock jumped in, adding, "Governor, if it is on Saturday morning, I feel sure that Bill Clark and I can orchestrate a rally for a few thousand TAC and TEA people around the state to be ready when you make your proclamation. It would be fun to see the hoorahs, excitement, tears of joy sending a strong signal to the rest of the world that Texans are united for our new Republic."

"Great! Good idea," Simmons replied. "That is something that we need to consider as we get closer to the day. Perhaps though, we should keep the actual date of the proclamation flexible until we know that we have everything in place. We can be more definite when I get the word from Della that we are set to go. We should tentatively plan on holding our final planning meeting on or about the 25th of February." Simmons continued. "Okay, that gives us just a couple of months to get it all together. Let's get started."

Gordon Giles waved his hand to get attention. "Governor, folks, two weeks from this Saturday my wife and I are putting on a real Texas barbeque at our San Antonio house for some friends. I would like to invite each member of this special group and their spouse to join us if you can. We'll be having some good Texas beef, country music and a great time. My secretary will follow up with formal invitations and directions. I hope all of you can come; it would be a good break for all of us."

A few muttered and nodded in response to Giles' invitation.

"Governor," Dan Stauffer called out softly, raising his hand. "Sir, even though many things are going through my mind at this time, count me in to assist wherever I can."

Governor Simmons taken by surprise, smiled and nodded slightly. "Thank you, *Governor*," and turned his attention toward Jacque Adams. "Della and, or Jacque, will remain your central point of contact, Dan, and they will keep you posted."

Jacque smiled confidently as she gathered up her materials and departed with the others.

The next morning the governor called Della to his private office. After coffee and exchange of pleasantries, Simmons looked directly at her. "Della, we are moving rather fast with our plan and at this point I would like your personal assessment of our members and their roles, commitment and their ability to see this through. I believe that more so than anyone you have a feel for whom we should consider an asset as well as those who may pose a liability at some point along the way. I know you won't hold back, so are you reasonably comfortable and, for that matter, confident that we have the all the right people on board with us?"

"Thank you, Governor," Della responded. "I have been paying close attention to the verbal and non-verbal behavior of all our members as I would if I were selecting them for a jury. I am sure you are aware as with any group of this size and varied backgrounds, that we have strong and weak links. Regarding specific individuals, I believe we have outstanding character and proven leadership in Generals Mitchell and Lawhorn. They are clearly up to the task at hand especially so now that can dedicate their full time to our project. I must say that while Manny Estrada says he is on board with us, I believe he could be persuaded to drift to the influence of others perhaps distracting from our mission. However, I don't think this will happen. As for Alex Mason, Governor, we both know that he is very religious; he is black and at some point in our final days, he could have second thoughts. However, I do expect him to stick with us."

"I agree , Della," Simmons nodded. "Please go on."

"My thought on Gordon Giles is that he is a true Texan at heart and will be a solid force throughout. His major motivation seems to be based on his conservatism; there is some hesitancy on my part to say that he conceptually or intellectually understands the true implications of what we are doing. However, he is a 'keeper'; he clearly understands the business environment and if we are in need of short-term money, he's the guy. I would say the same about Zach Hollis; his expertise in law enforcement is invaluable and he too has the Texas spirit so we can count on him. It appears to me that George Comstock and Bill Clark enjoy the fact that they have been able to arouse the emotions of thousands of people without understanding the true meaning of our secession goals. Again, we need them on board and I believe they will stick with us and see it through. And, now to Gene; Gene is a reasonably good PR guy; he is savvy and very dedicated to you, Governor. He will follow your lead and do his best to keep pace with events."

"I fully agree with you, Della, on all counts," the governor replied, "anything else?"

"There is one issue that concerns me," Della continued. "That is Dan Stauffer. I will put it straight; I have serious doubts about him and I think we should watch his moves closely. He has made his feelings known to our group while providing some indication of his cautious support. I don't know if he has restricted his feelings just to our members. He seems to be grudgingly going along with us, but his body language does not support his words. I do know that he and Jacque have struck up a friendly relationship and I have asked her to let me know if she discovers anything that might concern us. All in all and at this stage I believe we have little choice but to keep him on board, although with some trepidation on my part. That's how I see our group members, Governor. Of course, I could be off with any one of them, but feel fairly confident."

"No, I don't think so, Della," Simmons mused. "I agree with you, especially regarding Dan. You did not mention me in your assessments, Della?" he asked, smiling.

"No, sir, I didn't," she replied, returning the smile. "Let me be candid, Governor, there is no other person who I would ever hope to see or meet who surpasses your leadership, devotion, commitment, empathy and understanding of what the people of Texas need at this critical point in our history. With your heroic service in Vietnam, your terms as a representative, senator, lieutenant governor and now governor, we have admired you throughout and especially now. And, we so much appreciate your willingness to take on this great and noble cause for all who cherish freedom. None of us would want anyone else to lead us at this critical time. It is an honor and rewarding pleasure for me to be with you at this pivoting moment in the history of the Republic of Texas."

"Della, you are a patriot and I so much appreciate your kind words and your support. We both know that the outcome of our quest could be much different than what we intend. Like you and the others with us, I am willing to risk everything. Thank you, I will also add that it is you Della, who has served as an inspiring force during all of this. You are a true Texan and I am proud of your service and your support of this mission.

"Della you have been candid with me and now I will be with you. The central reason for our seceding has never been only about the president as I believe he is an honest man trying to do a job that he was ill prepared for; or solely about liberal or conservative causes, or the financial mess the U.S. now finds itself in. While these are very important issues, for me, it has always been about Texas and restoring our rights as an independent and sovereign nation so hard earned over our history. This has stuck with me since my childhood and first learning that I had distant cousins who fought and died at the Alamo and the Goliad massacre and in the battles along with General Sam Houston. Like many Texans, I also lost relatives in the Civil War. While fighting in the midst of battles in Vietnam, my mind was always wandering back to my home state of Texas while trying to insure that I would live through that mess and return to raise a family here. My mind, heart and soul are embedded here in this state and its fine people who appreciate our traditions and sacrifices. I love our music, our food, our culture and our way of life; having Texas free again is just about all I would ever want"

Della sat quietly listening with admiration for the patriot she knew the governor to be; he continued, "Della, does anyone except a native Texan truly understand just what it means to be a Texan? Probably not! I have traveled from Carthage to Leveland; from Brownsville to Sherman and to hundreds of other small cities and towns throughout our state. I know that within the heart and mind of most Texans they believe in God, hard work, self-sacrifice, personal freedoms, principles of morality and decency, military service and Peace Corps service, and family values like having a father and a mother, and local rule over federal rule. Being a Texan is a proud feeling found only in the tender most part of our hearts and in the tears we shed for those who paid the ultimate price for our freedom. Our legacy and conscience are found in their spilled blood and their sacrifice. As Texans, we know and honor our special heritage which was born during the seizure of the Alamo and from the thousands who have since died to protect our Texas way of life. Look at our Texas counties and cities; they are named after our patriots."

Reflecting a touch of melancholy and awkwardness, the governor smiled sheepishly and hesitated. "Oh well, enough of my sentimentality; let's get back to work. Della thanks again."

With moist eyes Della looked at Simmons. "Governor, I will remember those words for the rest of my life and my children will also come to know them as they were the most thoughtful, uplifting, heartfelt and inspiring words I have ever heard expressed. They all related to that which I also love...Texas. Our new Republic will be blessed to have you as its first president. Thank you, I am confident that we can only be successful in our quest to set Texas free. Thank you, Governor".

Della walked out of the door headed down the hallway and went outside of the capitol building and sat down on one of the stone pillars. Her heart was still beating fast; tears were streaming down her face forcing her to look away from people coming and going. She had never been so moved by such an open revelation by an individual for love of his country. How could she not be comforted knowing that she, too, felt the same! As the soft, warm winds of Austin blew across her tear stained face she remembered some of the tender moments of her own life. This was one of those moments and it would live forever in her heart.

Chapter Eleven

"**D**an, I believe we have two options," Jacque Adams said, exhaling slowly; her lips pursed. The formality between the co-conspirators had evolved comfortably to a friendly first name basis.

"The options, in my view, are quite simple;" she continued. "We can either blow their cover before Simmons attempts to carry out this ruse, or we can allow him to exercise his day in the sun and then bring the wrath of hell down upon him shortly afterward. What are your thoughts?"

Dan Stauffer sat listening thoughtfully to his energetic and fervent young colleague. This was their third such meeting, each after attending a session with the governor and the planning group. He finally spoke.

"Jacque, I agree; we need to move on this, but smartly and decisively. We can't afford to screw up any action we take; 'lest we become the victims and lose it all. Either of your options have the potential to not be successful if we don't carry it out properly. Tell me more about how you would suggest we go about sabotaging this *cockamamie* idiocy."

"In either approach," she quickly replied. "I suggest we develop a brief that would be delivered directly to the U.S. Attorney General in person. I can do that. In the brief 'before the act,' I would describe the treason that is about to be committed by the governor and a handful of zealous followers. I would explain that both you and I are loyal patriots to the United States and Texas, and if the governor is allowed to carry out his traitorous act, Texas, one of the, if not *the* wealthiest and richest state in the union, would be defiled, perhaps never fully recovering. I have a contact and would seek a personal audience with the AG and secure certain guarantees to benefit the two of us and others whom we favor. I have no doubt that both you and I will rise above this and become the preeminent leaders of Texas."

Speaking rapidly, she paused to seek an acknowledgment or comment from Stauffer. There was none; he sat stone-faced apparently listening intently. She continued, "If we decide to wait until after the Simmons' move, then it will be considerably trickier. We will need to have something in place with the administration to insure that you and I are not a part of the fiasco. I haven't thought that through yet; it will be difficult to advance something without giving it all away. On the other hand, if we are able to make our move before Simmons does, he will be caught red-handed and fully culpable for his act; your thoughts?"

Stauffer didn't respond immediately. Being the emblematic intellectual he was not one to move toward quick decisions. He finally spoke. "Jacque, I admire your logic and tenacity toward all of this. I am not one to provoke or quickly take to decisive actions. I do not agree with any of the uncanny thinking or what I believe to be personal greed that Simmons is demonstrating. Frankly, when I first learned of his scheme, my initial thought was this is a hoax or a pipe dream at most. I never ever thought it would reach the level that it now has. But, he and the secession actions must be stopped."

He mused silently for a moment before continuing, "Jacque, I believe both of your premises have merit and are quite accurate; if we wait until the deed is done, all hell will break loose and the two of us will be lost in the dust of the aftermath. If we take preemptive action we will have to insure that we get to the highest level possible in Washington with credible information or we will also suffer the consequences—there and here. I don't entirely seek the same goals as you; while I believe I can be an effective governor of this state and even beyond Texas, I don't have the same vigorous agenda as you, which I admire, by the way. So, I move we prepare a 'brief,' as you suggest; let's go over it thoroughly and insure that it is irrefutable, locked tight with evidence, and that it will get the attention at the necessary level in Washington. Then we must approach the U.S. Attorney General in such a way that we will not be brushed aside and lose the momentum or opportunity. As to the timing, I definitely believe we must be prepared to move *before* the act takes place. You create the presentation for both of us to review and we will then pursue ever so carefully the avenue or entrée to meet with the attorney general. Keep in mind, an audience with a lower bureaucrat won't work; the meeting has to be timely and personal with '*the man*.'"

"That's great, Dan!" she exuded. "Okay, I have a draft brief already written and will polish it up ASAP. I will also begin testing the water with a contact who I know I can trust who works in the AG's office. Now, to nurturing up a few prominent and trusted allies, I can name a few but need your support and development in this area. And again, we need to move fast on all that needs to be done before Simmons can preempt us."

Stauffer smiled slightly, "Jacque, you are a whiz; you are indeed the secret weapon that Della said you were. Get the draft paper back to me as soon as you can. I know at least a dozen or more in the House and the Senate who are not favored by our governor—nor were they of Shahan. I will contact them individually; not to reveal our plan, but lay the ground work for getting their support at the appropriate time. Let's plan on getting together, say Friday evening if your schedule permits and review the bidding. Meanwhile, we will play along with the game."

As Governor Simmons proceeded to think through his plan, the situation in Washington and around the world continued to play more in favor of his proposed secession action. The president, his associates and congressional democrats remained on a course of unbridled spending and legislating social changes. The banking and other financial institutions as well as the automobile industry bailouts had moved the country further into trillion dollar debts. The president's universal health care program was now being challenged by several state attorneys general. He was making eloquent speeches assuring the populace that he had the solution that would benefit everyone in every walk of life.

On the national security front, which was one of the major concerns of Governor Simmons and his planning group, North Korea boldly continued on its pathway to develop a nuclear weapons capability and threatening South Korea and recently shelled one of their small islands killing four people. They continued testing several medium range missiles by launching them over the Yellow Sea while the democrat establishment in Washington blithely went about business as usual. The president sent the secretary of state before the media to express his 'concern' and that the UN Security Council, involving China and Russia was the appropriate forum to address the issue. Concurrently, and in spite of protests and riots over the past fraudulent reelection of their tyrant leader, the Iranian militant government leaders continued with the pursuit of nuclear weapons grade plutonium development, persistent denouncing of Israel and testing the U.S. President's serenity.

The national debt continued to profusely grow and unemployment soared to an all time record. While the news media was forced to cover and report evolving domestic and international events, they did not challenge the president's seemingly awkwardness in bringing about the changes that were so often mentioned during his campaign.

During these challenging periods, the president himself, sat idly by making daily pronouncements of new and bigger programs; conducting press conferences and traveling about the country saying that he had the solution to our debt and unemployment problems. Meanwhile a docile America, the media, and the outside world stood by in virtual silence. The republican congress tried to fight back but thus far not with much success.

Several countries of the Middle East were in a state of uprising wanting change from the dictatorships and central rule by royal families that controlled their lives. The U.S. in response was one of a 'Johnny come lately' leaving many wondering where was the leadership in Washington.

The governor had also noted that his group of patriots had now completely shifted from a concern for illegals to that of protecting traditional values and way of life which Texans are so committed. This was now the catalyst for making his decision to take Texas into a free republic.

"Okay, Gene," Governor Simmons smiled; he was visibly pensive. "Let's see what you have scoped out. I am anxious to get the proclamation finalized, wrap up the details for our next meeting, set the date and proceed. Sit down."

"Yes, sir, thank you," Gene Todd replied as he handed the neatly paper clipped pages to the governor.

Simmons quickly thumbed the pages in packet. "You've really kept it brief, Gene," he said with a smirk. "Did you intend this to mimic the Gettysburg Address? I want to insure that I lay it all out—the why's, wherefores, necessity and imperatives of our commitment and decision. Is it all here?"

"Governor, I hope so," Todd replied confidently. "I, 'er, we, Attorney General Murphy, Jacque and I drafted the remarks and also ran them by Generals Mitchell and Lawhorn. The collective judgment is that your remarks should be as concise as possible; certainly to outline the events and situation in the country with the advent of the president and his extraordinary and radical economic and social policies and their impact on Texans. Sir, I believe we have fairly covered the issues and their impact; at least they are significantly outlined and highlighted. We thought your remarks should be timed at ten to no more than twenty minutes with a prompt exit by you. Otherwise, sir, the media hounds, those present and those observing on TV and radio will break away and begin their own speculating while you continued to speak. Those are our thoughts, sir."

"Okay, okay," Simmons fretted. "I know I am showing impatience. Let me get to your draft and I will get back to you. Thank you, Gene."

"Yes, sir," Gene Todd nodded and left the governor's office a little chagrined and disappointed with the meeting. He reported the event back to Della Murphy who suggested they just wait until the governor had read their suggested draft and go from there.

A few days later, Della Murphy literally burst into the governor's office unannounced. "Sir, forgive me," she said quickly as he looked up from his desk, surprised by the most unusual interruption.

Governor," Della blurted; her face flushed, "I am so distraught—embarrassed by what I must tell you that I can barely utter the words."

"What? What's happened, Della?" Simmons asked as he quickly rose from his chair and moved around the desk to face her. "Are you alright? What on earth? Sit down; catch your breath."

"Sir, I apologize for charging in here this way," she replied, now in a more calm voice. "Governor, a few weeks ago as a matter of security regarding the sensitivity of our planning activities, I had DPS security place telephone call-in call-out surveillance monitors on all the phones in my department. With all the different staff personnel and the ins and outs of people and activities, I wanted to make sure that we didn't have a snooper tagging me or any of our activities. You can call me overly cautious, but then I received a communications report last week and discovered that Jacque has been making numerous phone calls to Lt. Governor Stauffer from her private office phone and had received several in return. Sir, this breaks my heart and makes me furious at the same time to tell you that I also had a phone tap placed on her private office phone and on her home phone to record conversations. Just a bit ago, Zach Hollis brought a voice transcript to me and we listened together."

She paused and tears welled up in her eyes."Governor, I am sick to advise you that Jacque Adams and Dan Stauffer are conspiring to sabotage our secession plan. They have developed a paper divulging our plan, naming you as traitor along with the rest of us which they plan to deliver to the U.S. Attorney General just before our announcement date. She has told Stauffer that she has arranged for a private meeting with the AG which will be confirmed as soon as we complete our planning; thence she will fly to Washington and divulge it all a day or so before your announcement date. Again, sir, I am just too shocked to think clearly at the moment. I am so sorry, sir."

Simmons stood fast for a full minute, his mind racing. He finally walked over to the window and gazed down on the capitol grounds. "What is Zach's take?" he turned and asked.

"He suggests that we not make any sudden decisions or moves," she replied. "He would like to discuss a strategy with you before any actions are taken."

"Good; I agree," Simmons replied. "Okay, let's continue business as usual; keep a tab on our two *rats* and monitor their every conversation and move. I want to meet with Zach Hollis along with you here in my office in an hour; in the meantime, let me think this through."

"Yes, sir," Della sighed in response. "I am so sorry."

"So am I, Della," he replied shaking his head. "Keep Jacque and Stauffer in the loop as if all is well, provide no clue as to any announcement date or even imply to her that we have so much to do it may be delayed for several weeks so that she doesn't decide to make her trip to DC prematurely. See you in an hour."

"Yes, sir," she nodded.

Simmons returned to the draft proclamation that Gene Todd had left him, but couldn't concentrate. All sorts of notions and scenarios were running through his thoughts. *"How on earth can loyalty be so frivolously put aside? Dan Stauffer is not a surprise with his high and mighty intellect, but for Jacque to turn traitor against everything she professed to believe and supported. Unbelievable!"*

There was sharp rap on the door; his executive assistant entered and advised that the attorney general and Director, DPS, were there to see him.

"Have them come in," Simmons responded.

"Hi Zach, come in," he smiled half-heartedly. "Della and I have already had our brief discussion. What say you regarding this shocker?"

"Well, Governor, in my business I am never shocked at the untoward acts of people," Zach Hollis replied. "Surprised occasionally, but seldom shocked, Governor. Here's my suggestion if you will. First, I can put a watch tag on Jacque Adams with the security agents at the Austin-Bergstrom Airport and if and when she makes her move to go to DC, we will have her quietly detained for as long as necessary—even transport her to a holding facility here in town. She may scream for an attorney, but we can retain her on any number of charges."

"Okay, sounds good to me; Della?" Simmons replied, nodding.

"Zach and I have already discussed that scenario and I agree," Della replied. "We may break a few rules, but with what we are about to declare, I don't think they will matter much in the long run."

"Okay, fine," Simmons replied. "Go for it; now to our friend, the lieutenant governor, how do we manage him in the interim?"

"That could be either a big problem or one that simply goes away quietly until after we declare," Della said. "By that I mean, if he is not aware that Jacque has been incarcerated and believes she is off doing her deed, he may just sit tight and 'glow' waiting for the earth to crash down on the rest of us. We need to calculate the options; either leave him be to his own self confidence or have him arrested and held as we are her."

"Zach?" the governor looked to Hollis.

"Sir, after observing the lieutenant governor's demeanor throughout these weeks, his reticence, on again, off again behavior—arrogance, if you will, I believe we might just follow Della's notion to let him lie. I can put a couple of plain clothes rangers on him; watch his every move, continue to monitor his phones, disable his cell phone at the appropriate time, as well as Ms. Adams' cell phone, and maintain close surveillance. If he makes a move to step out of bounds, we will take him into custody."

"Good!" Simmons responded, brightening up somewhat. "You two put that plan in motion, keep it to just those who you need to involve, as I know you will, and Della as we discussed earlier, keep Jacque in the loop and ops normal, so to speak. God, I hate this! Sorry, just had to let it out."

He continued rapidly, "Okay, here's the deal; schedule our wrap-up meeting for this coming Sunday afternoon. I know that's a short string, but I believe we need to move out smartly. We will do it in the mansion; say three p.m. We will be secure enough there; nothing unusual about having a reception. I will have the staff put together a by invitation only notice. Della, make sure that Mitchell is ready with his plans. This is Tuesday, so that should be time to get ourselves all together."

He continued to ask questions and hand out directions. "Zach, how about you? You have been working with Mitchell—are you comfortable with where you are—ready to deploy and position your people?"

"Yes sir," Hollis responded. "We have a plan, we're organized and poised to move when directed to do so."

"Good, okay, then we will clean up everything Sunday and I want to set the proclamation for eleven a.m. the following Saturday. I don't believe we should delay any further; the timing should be right and historically so as well. I will have Gene begin the media preparations. As far as our Jacque and Dan are concerned, we will proceed as if they are right with us. I am sure, Zach, she will scamper like a rabbit to make travel plans as soon as we complete our meeting. You take it from there with your plan to nail her at the airport and monitor Stauffer as you discussed. I know this is moving a little fast, but under the circumstances, I believe we need to. Any questions?"

"No sir," both responded.

"Okay, I will be getting my proclamation remarks together and may call on you again before we have our wrap-up meeting; many thanks to the two of you."

Chapter Twelve

Della notified the planning team of the Sunday meeting, but did not divulge that the execution date had been set for the following Saturday.

Sunday came quickly and they all gathered at the governor's mansion as planned; after brief cordialities and the serving of cocktails and wine, Simmons had the room secured and opened the meeting.

"Thank you all for coming on such short notice," he began. "I hope to keep this gathering brief. I want to receive an update, first from General Mitchell and, in turn, from any of the planning staff, thence from Della and then Gene Todd, followed by discussion."

His tone and manner reflected anxiety and mild agitation. The latter obviously due to the presence of Jacque Adams and Dan Stauffer; both to whom he had forced pleasant greetings.

"Okay, General Mitchell," he continued. "Where are we?"

"Thank you, Governor," Mitchell began. "Sir, I believe we are set to go. Director Hollis and Tom Lawhorn have put it all together. Zach has his troopers and rangers are organized to deploy to the various highway junctures, airports and military installations, and Tom has established coordination with the national guard commanders, alerting them for mobilization on call. George Comstock and Bill Clark have organized and coordinated their TAC rally to kick off promptly after your proclamation declaration. Our Command Center in the capitol building is up and ready to activate on a few hours' notice. Your staff and technician support has been superb. I will be pleased to have Zach, Tom, George or Bill discuss in detail their activities if you wish; otherwise, I am confident that we can execute at your call.

"Thank you, Chris," Simmons responded. "That's excellent! No, I don't need to get into *nitty gritty* micro managing. You have laid out a comprehensive plan and you're the experts. If questions arise later, we can address them; Della."

"Thank you, Governor," Della began. "I have only to say that I believe we are ready to go. As I have kept you briefed daily, Manny Estrada and I have thrown a broad net over the legislative body; brought several trusted members into our confidence with exceptional support promised. I have also drafted a Republic of Texas court system plan to include proposed member candidates; Zach Hollis has created a republic security and law enforcement organization structure plan which you have reviewed. As you are aware, we are prepared to establish martial law if deemed necessary in the aftermath of the announcement. There a million other 'nits and lice' details which I am prepared to discuss as you wish."

"Good, Della," he smiled. "Thank you! Gene?"

"Governor, I have a media notification plan in place which addresses TV, radio and newspapers. I will need a few hours 'heads up' to scramble the lead outlets to be present for your announcement. In that regard, the major Houston, Dallas-Ft. Worth, San Antonio, El Paso, Lubbock and Amarillo media agencies all have stringers here in Austin; so we will be prepared to get near instant maximum state coverage. We will no doubt be inundated with the major cable news channels who will want to get to you soonest. In that regard, I have a media query response plan which you have reviewed. I suggest, sir, following your announcement you take cover and retreat to your office or the Command Center to monitor and evaluate the reaction. You will, without a doubt, be receiving more phone calls than you can manage. Many of those calls will be bogus and not the person represented on the line. I have informally briefed the capitol switchboard supervisor as a routine to screen your calls and will re-brief her just before your announcement. Lastly, you have the draft proclamation which we prepared; can we assist you any further with it?"

"Thank you, Gene, good run down," the governor replied. "And no, I have about wrapped up the proclamation. You folks did a good job with it; I just hope I can deliver equally as well. Okay, comments, questions from anyone?"

After a pause, Dan Stauffer held up his hand. "Governor, what sort of timing are we looking at to kick this off?"

"Good question; I was about to get to that most critical part of our meeting," Simmons replied with a smile. He slowly scanned his colleagues and without further hesitation, responded: "My intention is to announce the proclamation this coming Saturday morning, February 20th, at eleven a.m. central time.

The room was dead silent at first and then the team members began to look around and eye one another, some smiling while others sat still waiting for further reaction. The reality of the moment and all they had discussed, planned and looked forward to was suddenly here.

Governor Simmons, Della and Zach Hollis subtly focused on Jacque Adams and Dan Stauffer for their reaction. Jacque was obviously moved by the governor's abrupt announcement of the proclamation date. She sat upright and turned her head toward Stauffer. He remained stolid looking straight ahead without displaying any reaction to the pronouncement, nor did he make eye contact with Jacque Adams. It was apparent that she was visibly disturbed. This was late Sunday afternoon with only five days for her to carry out the plan that she and Stauffer had concocted. She knew that she had to move fast, find a way to make an excuse to be away from Della's office to fly to Washington. Not expecting the proclamation to occur so soon, a multitude of thoughts and options were obviously whirling around in her head.

"Well my friends, fellow Texans, the time has come," Simmons spoke after a brief moment, permitting his announcement to settle in before breaking the silence in the room. "Our plans are completed, we will have the next few days to make final adjustments and execute on Saturday. I urge, no demand, the same secrecy that has allowed us to complete our actions. I applaud each of you for your commitment, hard work and support. God bless Texas and God bless each of you!"

He then motioned to Gene Todd to open the door that led back into the luxurious room where they had first enjoyed their cocktails and wine; two wait staff members were waiting to serve drinks. When all had been served, the governor held his glass high and in a confident voice pronounced, "God bless Texas; our Texas!"

Except for Dan and Jacque, who were sullen faced, the others responded in kind with accompanying gleeful shouts.

∽

The next few days were destined to be busier than ever. Chris Mitchell held daily meetings with his key people; Lawhorn, Hollis, Comstock and Clark went about getting everything ready for Saturday morning. Likewise, Della and Manny Estrada continued to make contacts with trusted legislative members while the governor and Gene Todd worked on his proclamation remarks. Della kept a close eye on Jacque's movements and demeanor; the latter of which was cool, but seemingly focused on the tasks at hand. "She's a good *actress*," Della noted to herself.

Zach Hollis reported back to Della late Tuesday that he had recorded only two brief conversations between Jacque Adams and Dan Stauffer. In each, he said, Stauffer seemed guarded in his comments and responses.

"Not in a negative sense," Hollis said, "just more subdued than before the last meeting. He is a quirky one." He continued, "Okay, here's her plan; she has made reservations out of Bush International in Houston for DC tomorrow night and has scheduled an appointment for early Thursday morning with her AG contact. She told Stauffer not to worry; she knew how to finesse getting away from her office to make the trip."

"Hmmm, that's interesting," Della responded. "She has been working right along, putting on a good act and hasn't mentioned anything to me thus far. This will be interesting. If she is apparently going to drive to Houston and depart from there, are you prepared to detain her at that point?"

"You bet," Hollis replied. "We have her flight number, time and so forth; so we will collect her there and hold her incognito in Houston until the weekend, then make some determination regarding our next move after that. Do you agree?"

"Yes," Della replied, nodding her head. "What about Stauffer?"

"Well, so far he hasn't made any untoward moves and my guess is that he will sit tight and wait for Jacque's DC plan to kick in, which it won't of course; neither will they be able to communicate with one another. I suspect being the *cool cat* he thinks he is, Stauffer will go along with whatever takes place—wondering what happened to his partner. I don't see any need to take him in unless and until he gives us cause. You legal folks can deal with him after everything else takes place. It will be interesting to see if Ms. Adams spills the beans against him thereafter."

"Okay, Zach," Della sighed. "Thank you. I will brief the governor and keep you posted on her moves here, her disappearance or whatever."

Della did not have to wait very long. The next day was Wednesday and Jacque Adams knocked twice sharply on Della's office door and walked in. "Maam, Della, I am sorry to interrupt; I have an emergency; my father has had a heart attack in Houston. I know this couldn't happen at a worse time, but I must go to him. Once I see him and it appears that he is recovering, I will get back as soon as possible. I am so sorry; I know you need me here!"

Della played along. "Oh Jacque," she said, standing and moving around the desk to hug her. "Go, and go now. Will you drive or fly over there?"

"I can drive quicker than messing around with getting a flight and it's a short trip," she replied. "I will keep in touch and return as soon as possible. Thank you and good luck with all you have to do." She departed.

Della reported the event to both Hollis and the governor, sighed deeply and went back to work. "*That's done,*" she sighed to herself. "*God help us through this!*"

Zach Hollis later reported that Jacque had been apprehended on Wednesday afternoon as she drove into the Houston airport. Wednesday, Thursday, and Friday came and went without further incident. On Thursday, under the guise of a security exercise, the governor activated the Texas National Guard which was immediately deployed to designated spots along the border and other key important points. Friday morning, Zach Hollis checked to insure that his district commanders were in position to briefly close the Interstate and other major highways at the moment of Governor Simmons secession speech. Della worked diligently on legal and legislative issues the new Republic would face in the upcoming days. All had their mind on Saturday morning wondering just what the reaction would be in Texas and other states. The governor had met with Della and General Mitchell on two occasions during this time wanting to make sure all possibilities were attended to. Friday evening as he thought of the Alamo, Goliad, Colonel Travis, and other episodes of Texas history, he was confident that he was ready to begin the odyssey as the new president of the Republic of Texas.

Chapter Thirteen

Governor Bill Simmons was awake before dawn on Saturday morning, S-day. This would be the most important day of his life. Not any previous event, including combat in Vietnam, had ever had him more keyed-up. He had rehearsed his remarks over and over; they were cemented firmly in his mind. There would be *no* teleprompter in use for him today, or any day, for that matter. He was ready. He eased out of bed so as not to disturb his wife and slipped downstairs for coffee.

On Friday the day before, Della had informed him that Jacque Adams was taken into custody in Houston two nights before as she prepared to board a flight to Washington D.C. She would be held for further disposition until after everything settled down following the governor's announcement. Dan Stauffer was still under close surveillance by the Texas rangers; no doubt he was extremely pensive having not heard anything from Jacque. The governor had issued his final instructions to Gene Todd the evening before.

"The media is yours," he said. "Exercise your plan as you see fit. You don't need to consult me further. Also, please advise the others on our team that I wish to be left to myself in the morning; no interruptions short of an invasion."

At ten o'clock he departed the mansion, waved off his driver and began a casual stroll over to the capitol building. The weather was spring-like and beautifully fresh. A few cars moved about the streets and then he noticed that TV outlet trucks and vans had begun to be positioned near the front steps of the capitol.

"They are eager for a Saturday morning; must be a slow news day," he chuckled to himself. So as not to be recognized, he quickly diverted his path to enter a side entrance door of the capitol. As he pondered his morning schedule he knew this day would be a remarkable moment in his life; he felt good and confident. After insuring the Command Center was fully activated and his key people in place, his primary thought was that Texas would now regain control of its destiny as God intended.

At eleven o'clock sharp, Governor Simmons stepped out onto the red marble portico just above the broad steps leading up to the front entrance of the capitol building of the state of Texas. The capitol grounds were bare with only a few pedestrians walking casually about. He stepped up to the lectern now surrounded by a bank of microphones, he noticed that Speaker Estrada and Representative Alex Mason were standing nearby along with two state troopers. Several video camera operators were squatted down below on the steps. Standing alone, he looked much taller than his six feet. He quickly scanned the entire group setting immediately before him, the manicured grounds and the expanse of the city of Austin; and then looked directly at the cameras.

"My fellow Texans," he began in a strong and much rehearsed confident voice. "This moment and this day will become a landmark in the history of the great state of Texas. The United States has been in turmoil for several years and especially so during these past two plus years. We witnessed the most overworked and overplayed political campaign for president of the United States in our history and the scenario still persists and continues non-stop. Texas and Texans have become the unfortunate beneficiaries of multiple promises made and promises being enacted into federal law. The president has made it clear that more is yet to come. I strongly believe that most of these changes are not appropriate for Texans, our history, and our way of life."

"In my few minutes with you on this beautiful Texas day, I do not intend to rant, rave or shout about what might have or even should have happened in our country. However, I do want to briefly review where we are at this time, not necessarily where it was promised that you would be now or in the foreseeable future, it's where you and we are on this day. *Hope and Change, Change you can believe in*, that 's the mantra you have heard for nigh on three years. Hope and change from what to what we must ask. The President of the United States has been in office for almost a full term and there is the likelihood that he will be reelected for a second term. For whatever reasons which may include his lack of self-confidence, ability, strength, knowledge, experience, guidance, direction, he continues to ply the airways and orchestrate public hearings with speeches that make a public case for more social legislation of which do not fit well with our Texas traditions. As an example, the president and his democratic congress have already passed the don't ask, don't tell act, allowing for gays to serve openly in the military. Their eyes are now on making it a federal law giving the right for gays to marry. The president recently said that his justice department will not defend the federally mandated 'marriage act.' My concern here is that they have paid no attention to how Texans feel about these issues.

"The man in the White House on this day, if he is actually there and not out making another promissory speech, was elected to office by less than one third of the states in the Union. But that is not at issue, he was duly elected by the established process of the majority vote. He won the necessary votes from the populous states that believed in the chant for *Change*. Permit me to quickly review what the *Change* and promises agenda has brought us. First and foremost, the change in the White House has provided us with a man who has not a whit of experience in managing, leading, guiding or directing *any* activity of note, business venture of any size or a precinct, county or state. Yet, he is the president of these United States, who in his period of office has managed to plunge the nation into a great economic debacle while increasing threats to our national security. Experts now tell us that our national debt approaches fifteen trillion dollars. He likewise threw many billions of so-called stimulus and bailout money to many institutions. These stimulus packages were supposed to have resulted in raising employment levels; however, our unemployment rate is nearing ten percent. You may recall when job losses reached eight percent under the previous administration, the democrats screamed to high heaven along with the media. Have you heard any major complaints or media outcry about the ten percent unemployment rate? Of course you haven't, because we are still waiting for the various stimulus *changes* to kick in.

"You will recall the campaign promise regarding 'earmarks.' Remember the candidate who told us that he would personally scrub every bill placed on his desk and name the congressional culprits who inserted expensive and greedy projects. Have you heard about the now labeled, 'brothel train' that will run from Disneyland to Vegas and the senator from Nevada who 'earmarked' that mega-billion project to an innocuous bill? No, you haven't, nor will you be informed of billions upon billions of other dollars of your tax money being shoveled out frivolously by members of congress and signed off by this president."

"Let's quickly review his national healthcare initiative. I presume you are all aware that congress has exempted themselves from the president's healthcare plan; are you also aware that the national unions are exempted as well and will be free to force the respective industries to provide their workers with healthcare? Several pro-democrat states have also been given waivers or exceptions to this new plan. These, my fellow Texans, are not only changes you can believe, they are changes that are wrecking our country and your families included, unless, of course, *YOU* are a congressman or a national union worker.

"Now let me turn to the one single element that sustains our country—the single most important element, if you will—national security. How frequently do you hear or have you heard the term, 'national security,' mentioned in this administration? Of course, not often! It appears to be the last item on the list of presidential priorities and his congress. We do know that this administration would like to get rid of the 'Patriot Act' which, if successful, would make it more difficult to track down alleged so-called 'lone wolf' terrorists such as the one recently discovered near the city of Lubbock. During the campaign, it was easy to promise closing the Guantanamo terrorist prison facility as soon as he was elected. No one asked, what about the dangerous prisoners being held there; where would they go? As it turns out none of those supporting the closure of this upscale prison facility want the terrorist suspects in their home states—not even the president's home state. So to work toward keeping his promise, he quietly 'solves' the problem by bribing small nation states to take them! Four terrorist prisoners were sent to the island of Palau along with twenty million of your tax dollars; five were sent to Bermuda along with an 'undisclosed' amount of your tax dollars. Again, where was the media outrage? These payoffs, alone, is more than sufficient cause to keep them incarcerated and isolated at Guantanamo. It now seems that the president has come around to where he is accepting this logic.

"My friends, without national security over our land and our people, we can forget any other wishes and desires. We are presently being taunted by North Korea and Iran and somewhat minimized by Russia; all are testing our tolerance and our will to see how far they can push us, and we are witnessing they are just about having their way while this White House sits and hopes these potential threats will just go away, or perhaps be persuaded to be nice, or in some cases bought off. And, just a few months ago, the nation of Egypt was in crisis; hundreds of thousands of their citizens took to the streets to protest central government oppression and they have now taken back control of their country. Several other Middle Eastern countries are now following Egypt's example and, most unfortunately, not the example that the U.S. could have offered by quickly and openly providing support to the people of Egypt, Libya, Syria, Yemen, Jordan, Tunisia, and Bahrain. They are accomplishing this by sheer people power willing to put their lives on the line and most certainly not from the White House who stayed busy sending mixed signals regarding its concern for their plight. While Washington attempted to 'game' the uprising of people in the Middle East thousands were being killed while many countries throughout the world watched, waited and listened for an effective response from the U.S. But no clear supporting voice came from the U.S. We here in Texas looked upon these protesters with admiration and pride for what they are doing and that was they wanted their freedom. Thus far, the president's only apparent open strategy is one of mixing words and actions relying on NATO and other European nations to take the lead, all being done to conform to domestic politics insuring another term in office. No, this president has for the most part left national security behind; addressing it only when nations in the Middle East take action by themselves, or perhaps when the commanding general in Afghanistan mentions it in the media and is then fired. To most observers, it is clear that since this president took office the reputation and prestige of the United States in the world community has fallen to an all time low.

The oppression of people by a government designed to keep them from being what their democratic traditions and culture demand is not just found in the Middle East, but much more closer to home where Washington's liberal government policies are altering the landscape for those who want to retain traditional values and customs, especially here in Texas. And it is time to fight back— and sooner, rather than later! This president appears to be focused solely on his take on socio-economic issues. He views the United States as a place where his social experiments can and should take place as well as his piggy bank in which he can go to for any amount on any given day and spend it as he wishes under the guise of a stimulus; notwithstanding the fact that *it is your* money in that bank. And, when that bank is empty, he has plans for you to replace it—with every conceivable tax scheme he can think of. Let me quickly add, my remarks have been directed toward the president; however, he is in no way alone in this decline and destruction of America; he is surrounded by a group of the shrewdest career congressional politicians, lobbyists, and bureaucrats in the world, as well as manipulative advisors. They are not only willing accomplices, they are also with equal guilt in creating and perpetrating this evolving social and economic disaster and in many cases both of the major political parties share the blame.

"Now, I want to turn to Texas, your Texas and mine.

The concerns I am sharing with you this day are not only about the president, or solely about his liberal causes, or the financial mess we now find ourselves in. Yes, these are critically important issues and growing more so daily, but it's about Texas and sustaining our rights as an independent and sovereign people so hard earned over our history. Here in Texas, we love our traditional way of living and do not want any part of Hollywood, Boston, New York City, or the many social changes coming from Washington DC. As your governor, I will not sit idly by and let Texas values and traditions be taken away from us.

"As Texans we know and honor our special heritage which was born during the seizure of the Alamo and from the thousands who have since died to protect our Texas way of life. Our legacy and conscience are found in their spilled blood and their sacrifice. Many of your fathers, mothers and grandparents planted, plowed and picked cotton, corn, and potatoes in our Texas fields to sustain us through hard times putting food on our tables. They did not sit around drawing welfare checks and having more children to take even more from the government, or I should say, our purse. They must be turning over in their graves at the mess we now find ourselves in.

"Our proud heritage, commitment and hard work have provided

our state and our people with self determination and independence from virtually any and all outside requirements. Let me remind you; we are the largest producer of agricultural food products, dairy products and oil and gas energy. We manufacture virtually every product required for living comfort. Our banking and financial institutions are rock solid. We have the largest and most modern hospitals and health care facilities in the nation and the world. Our transportation systems match any others anywhere. We have the greatest and most diverse education system in the world. Our secondary school systems and our colleges and universities are unmatched; along with research institutions that are world renowned. And, we have no state income tax. Finally, I am pleased to tell you and the nation today that we currently have upwards of a ten billion dollars surplus in our state reserve coffers; this compared to equal and greater deficits within many, if not most, of those states that committed their votes for the '*hope and change you can believe in* president' we have in the White House."

A large crowd of curious on-lookers had now begun to gather on the capitol grounds. Many had strolled over from the sidewalks while others had picked up the governor's speech on the radio and drove over to see what was going on.

"My fellow Texans," he continued. "A progressive socialist cancer is moving across the United States and will soon completely engulf our state as it already has others causing Texans to accept laws that crush our traditions and way of life. This spreading malignancy will demand that we give up our traditions as well as redistribute all our resources, wealth and well-being and forced to share everything we have with those who have frivolously taxed and wasted theirs away. Are we, as Texans, ready to give up all that our ancestors fought for and which we have earned and thoughtfully managed for our present and our future?"

There was a small chorus of "No's" that began to rumble through the growing crowd. The governor held up his hand to call for quiet and continued.

"During the past few months a group of well-informed, thoughtful and committed Texans—lawmakers, businessmen, senior national defense officers, law enforcement, educators and laymen— have been meeting with me to address all that I have shared with you today and I honored and pleased to advise all Texans and those across the

United States that Texas does not approve nor will we any longer accept the dictatorial and socialistic and tradition changing policies of the President of the United States, his administration, or the congress. At twelve o'clock noon today, the 20th day of February, I will formally advise the President of the United States that Texas is declaring its constitutional and God-given rights to independence. I will advise him that by the authority vested in me as Governor of the Great State of Texas, I hereby declare that Texas is seceding from the United States of America on this date and establishing its rightful independence as the Republic of Texas. Until elections are held later this year, I will assume the role of President of the Republic of Texas. May God Bless each of you and may God Bless Texas!"

The crowd of less than a hundred which had gathered on the capitol grounds was at first hushed and then broke into indistinguishable screams, shouts and hand clapping. A bevy of Texas Rangers immediately moved out onto the portico and formed a line between the governor and several TV cameramen, reporters and others who attempted to get near him for pictures and to ask questions. Two rangers escorted Simmons to the capitol building; while Gene Todd moved to the lectern two rangers lowered the U.S. flag and raised the Lone Star flag of Texas.

"Ladies and Gentlemen," Gene attempting to raise his voice above the chaotic noise. "Please...listen for just a moment. For the media, our new soon to be president, William Simmons, will not address any questions at this time. I will inform you of the time and place at which he will meet with you in a formal press conference. I have copies of his just completed remarks if you will come see me up here. Thank you all for coming and God Bless the Republic of Texas on this momentous day!

Now I would like to give the lectern to Speaker Estrada who has a few words to say."

"Mi amigos (in Spanish), the words of incoming President Simmons are important to all of us who hold dearly our Spanish heritage and our history as being Tejanos in this great land that we have called our home for hundreds of years. Washington would try to make us rethink our way of living, our belief in God and family. I could not stand by and let this happen. With my presence as a senior member of his team, our Republic of Texas President has assured me that our new nation will be fully shared by all and that no one will be a second class citizen. You can count on me to keep this promise as we go forward. God bless Tejas and God bless each of you. Gracious; and I will now ask our Texas Representative Alex Mason to address you and our new nation."

Alex seemed hesitant for a moment then he strolled up to the lectern. "Thank you, Speaker Estrada. Many of you are wondering why I am standing here giving my recognition and support to our new nation, the republic of Texas and to its president. Well, I will be brief; suffice it to say that I have had enough of the liberalism and socialism coming out of Washington that is being imposed on those of us who hold strong religious, patriotic, and traditional convictions. I ask all groups to join me in supporting President Simmons as he prepares to lead a new nation back to God, reconfirming our basic values and into untold glory for all of us. This is not a black, brown, or white thing; it is a destiny thing, a preservation of ideals, and something that promotes the aspirations and future of all Texans. Thank you for your support and God bless the Republic of Texas on this special day!"

Manny and Alex then joined Simmons and Gene Todd and they departed for the Command Center to meet the others. His entire team was present and hovered around the several television sets which had been installed to monitor the various network and cable news reporting. Caught off guard on an 'off news' day, it was apparent that the news media was scrambling to characterize the earth-shattering story: "renegades," "traitors," "*patriots,*" "breakaway republic," "defectors," "cowboys," depending on the news network, each had its own portrayal of the secession announcement. Texas had caught the entire country, and the world for that matter, by surprise causing an unexpected shock. The initial coverage ranged from praise to denouncement to condemnation.

The governor knew he had to make a call to the president. It would be no less courteous to do so, but before he could move to the quiet of his office to make the call, his secretary informed him that the secretary of state was on the phone. He was ready; he had prepared himself to address whichever U.S. government official, including the president who came first.

"Madam Secretary," he responded. "Bill Simmons. I had fully intended to initiate the call first, but I thank you. Let me please say upfront, I offer no apology or detailed explanation at this time. You have been briefed or provided my remarks and our rationale for today's announcement. It should therefore come as no surprise to you or the president." He paused to hear the response.

There was at first silence and then, "Governor Simmons, you have made a grave and reprehensible error in judgment," she began. "You have violated the Constitution of the United States of America. By making such a dire fool of yourself and the people of your great state, you have committed treason against the United States of America. I am dispatching officials from my office to meet with you as soon as they are prepared to depart. In the meantime, the president and I beseech you to immediately retract your statement to the people of Texas and the nation, for their own good, peace of mind and yours, Sir. I..."

"Madam Secretary," Simmons interrupted. "First, do not bother to send any of your staff here to see me or my people. They will be apprehended and returned to Washington. Second, Madam Secretary, my pronouncement today is the culmination of months of research, study and deliberation. Texas and Texans are united in this action and we are proceeding to bring official status to our republic. Next week, my secretary of state will be available to work with you and your staff at your pleasure. Good day and thank you for your call."

Simmons returned to the main room of the Command Center to confer with his team, a little unnerved by the call, but to proceed with the multitude of decisions and actions that lay before him. The capitol switchboard immediately became swamped and the operators worked diligently to work through the myriad of incoming calls, permitting those that could be verified as legitimate to placed on priority hold. The governor took them in order; the first from the governor of Oklahoma.

"Bill, damn you've got guts!" the Oklahoma governor exclaimed. "When in the hell did you come up with this scheme? Are you in this by yourself? Who's with you? What do you think those bureaucrats in Washington will do?" He continued with a barrage of questions. "Why didn't you cut me in?"

"Hold it, Brad," Simmons interrupted. "Hey, we, my staff of loyal and committed Texans, have been working at this for weeks, months. We have had enough of this charade developing in Washington. Even though this has been building for several years, this president and his gang of socialists and change agents who can't shoot straight are more than we can take down here in our state. I presume you have heard my remarks, or about them anyway; if not get the transcript and let's discuss soon. As you can imagine, I am in overload; thank you, good friend, for calling and I will call you back soonest. God bless."

Governor Simmons hung up and pushed the next incoming call. It was the governor of Wyoming—the urgent questions were the same—Simmons was patient as he continued taking calls from Louisiana, Wyoming, Nebraska, Hawaii and even a few from the UK and Germany. After an hour and half or so, he took a break and called Gene Todd.

"Gene," he began, "put together a fact sheet; coversheet, if you will, prepared for my signature and attach it to my secession statement. I will review and sign it and then dispatch it as soon as you can by the fastest means to this list of state governors; prepare multiple packages for later mailing. Oh, and prepare the same packages in Spanish for dispatch to the President of Mexico and each of the Mexican border state governors."

"Yes, Sir," Gene responded. "I'll have a draft for you shortly."

Simmons then summoned Chris Mitchell to accompany him to his Command Center private office and to bring along Zach Hollis, Tom Lawhorn and Della.

Once they were all gathered inside the office, he closed the door. "Sit down, please," he looked around, nodding. "How are things going, Chris?" he asked.

"So far, so good, Governor," Mitchell began. "As you know, we had previously contacted each of the major military facility commanders in the state advising them of a pending exercise relating to Homeland Security. I gave each of them my number here in the Command Center should they have any questions as things progressed. I also advised them that DPS officers accompanied by a national guard officer would arrive at their main gates when the exercise kicked-off. Zach will brief you further that his troopers along with at least one guard officer is in place, but interestingly, I have not received a single call from any of the military facility commanders since your announcement. I will add that no doubt the lines back to their respective military headquarters are buzzing off the wall. Let me bring Zach Hollis into the conversation and then Tom Lawhorn will give you a guard update—Zach."

"Thanks, Chris," Zach Hollis acknowledged. "Governor, as Chris has briefed you, my DPS guys each accompanied by a ranger are in place at each of the military facilities throughout the state. Additionally, as planned, we deployed troopers to all major and several busy minor highway entrances into Texas. Thus far there have no reported incidents and we have not inhibited any traffic flow and all appears normal. As you would expect, several of our deployed troopers have been met by highway patrol officers from border states at some locations. Most, of course, had heard about your announcement and are naturally curious. Each of our folks has a prescribed statement to provide anyone who has questions. The statement simply says that we are in 'ops normal' and we anticipate there should be no interference in traffic flow; at least for the time being."

"Thank you, Zach," Simmons replied in a solemn tone. "Tom, how are things with the Guard; any word from Washington through your channels?"

"As Chris said, Governor, so far, so good," Tom Lawhorn responded. "As has been reported, we are working closely with both DPS and the Texas Rangers around the state. We are also working with the Border Patrol, and while they take their orders from Washington, they are being very cooperative. I personally briefed each region commander up and down the border on Friday; told them that an impending exercise of considerable magnitude would soon be taking place and that it may conflict with what Washington and Homeland Security agrees to. They each acknowledged and didn't question me further. Additionally, there has been no unusual activity along the border; of course it's early in the game. Regarding Washington, I have had no word from the Chairman, Joint Chiefs, so I guess I still have my retirement check." They all chuckled. "But, maybe not for long!" he quickly added.

"Well, thank you all," Simmons replied soberly.

"Sir," Gene Todd interrupted, knocking on the door; opening it slightly. "I am sorry to interrupt Governor; the White House just announced that the president will go on the air at three p.m. our time with a statement. He's at Camp David and will be making the broadcast from there."

"Okay," Simmons responded with nod. "That's about an hour and a half from now...should be interesting. Okay anything else; Della?"

"No Sir, except what should we do with Jacque Adams?" she asked. "I presume we still have her being held in Houston; is that right, Zach?"

"Yes, that's correct," Zach Hollis replied. "She is in the custody of the Houston police and isolated from everyone else. I am advised that since your announcement she appears to be in a state of shock; she won't talk or eat. They are watching her closely as a potential suicide case. She hasn't spoken to anyone since we arrested her. Now that the word is out, we do need to take some action with her."

"What do you propose?" Simmons promptly asked.

"The simple solution, Governor, er, Mr. President" Zach began, "just release her to her own recognizance. There is little harm, if any, she can cause the project now. That would be my recommendation; perhaps offer her any assistance she may desire, permit her to return here, obviously clear out personal effects from her office and let her go. I could put a tail on her for a while if desired, but I wouldn't think even that is necessary. I think she is a whipped canary."

Governor Simmons looked at Della. "What say you?"

Della shrugged, "fine with me. I agree with Zach, I see little harm she can do now, but perhaps we should be concerned about the possibility of her going off the deep end; committing suicide or worse, doing harm to someone else. Then there is the next issue, that of our 'Lt. Governor'?"

Simmons sat for a moment mulling over the situation; finally speaking. "Okay, Zach, if you believe Jacque Adams is of no harm to herself or someone else, then tomorrow morning release her. But, as a minimum, you may attempt to debrief her if she is willing to talk, if not so be it. On the other hand to play it safe, why don't you call in a psychiatrist to have a look at her before we turn her loose on the street.

"Okay, I'll contact Houston," Zach replied, "and have 'em run her through a psych exam before they release her."

"You may also offer her escort back to Austin if she wishes such," Simmons mused. Now to Dan Stauffer, any ideas?"

No one spoke at first, and then Della responded. "Well, he's sitting out there wondering what we're doing in here. I am sure he saying to himself, 'I'm the Lt. Governor of this state and being treated like a leper.' And, leper he is. On the other hand, while he is a traitor to our cause here, aided and abetted Jacque Adams in her pursuit to sabotage our historic move toward freedom, he has done nothing overtly to interfere. Weird he may be and virtually of no value to our cause, I say, Governor, we move promptly to confirm you President of the Republic of Texas and ease him out of the picture."

"No equivocating on your part, Della," Simmons smiled. "What say the others of you? Incidentally, where is Manny? My oversight by not having him join us here. Della, would you mind inviting him to come in."

"Yes, Sir," she replied; departing the office.

"Coffee anyone while Della is fetching Manny?" Simmons offered.

As each moved to retrieve a cup of coffee, Della returned with Speaker Manny Estrada.

"Ah, come in Manny," Simmons greeted. "Let me apologize, strictly a hasty oversight on my part, Manny, in trying to get a feel for the reactions around the state and the country. Please join us. I have just posed a question regarding the disposition of Lt. Governor Stauffer. Permit me to preface that with disturbing, even damning information which I don't believe you are fully aware of, if at all."

Simmons continued. "Briefly, Manny, Dan Stauffer has been a traitor to our cause and efforts. He and our 'trusted' Jacque Adams have over weeks created a plan to reveal our secession plan to the U.S. Attorney General with the intent of indicting all of us. Fortunately, Della discovered the scheme and we intercepted Jacque before she was able to sabotage our pronouncement for secession. That's it. Jacque has been retained in isolation by the police in Houston and as you are aware, Stauffer is in the other room. He's a good actor, but he must be a bundle of chaotic nerves inside, wondering what is taking place with no word from Jacque and being left out of our discussions. There, you have it. I know this likely comes as a shock; so now we have to decide how we work with our lieutenant governor."

The Speaker of the House sat for a moment, not appearing to be overly surprised by the governor's revelation. He spoke finally. "Sir, this doesn't shock me; Dan Stauffer is an enigma. He is extremely bright, thoughtful and a deep thinker, but he is not, nor has he demonstrated any obvious loyalty to this state, you, this plan, or anything else except himself and his personal goals. It is time to get him out of the way. Sir, permit me ask what is our next step regarding organizing our new government? I presume that we are going to move forward quickly, confirm you as President of our new Republic, establish a cabinet and move on? All that being the continuation of our plan, then we simply leave Dan Stauffer to his own devices."

"So you are suggesting we ignore his previous misdeeds and ease him out quietly?" Simmons mused. "Interesting, thank you; Della agrees. Now, about getting on with organizing the government of the Republic of Texas, each of you, including our entire planning group, has indicated that I, for at least the time being, assume the office of President of the Republic. Thank you for your trust and I am prepared to do just that. We can formalize the appointment as soon as Della sets up the process. Thereafter, I will seek the counsel of each of you in filling the necessary chairs of responsibility. Do each of you agree?"

"Hear, hear," they all cheered in unison.

"Thank you, my friends," Simmons smiled and nodded humbly. Looking at his watch he noted, "It's almost time for the President of the United States to pronounce sentence upon us. Let's get back into the control center and all listen together; God bless Texas!"

As they departed the office, George Comstock entered the control room. "Governor, I am sorry I have been out of pocket, but I have been checking on our Tea Party rallies. And in a word, they are in full swing around the state and here in Austin especially. The police estimate that we have five thousand or more marching and chanting up Congress Avenue, and spreading off into the side streets and parks. That also goes for Houston, Dallas, Fort Worth, El Paso, Amarillo and over in East Texas at Texarkana. People are on fire with your announcement and the 'down with this government's social programs' signs tell the story. Bill Clark is on the phones coordinating with our TAC centers. I'll keep you posted."

"That's great, George," Simmons patted him on the back; we just want to be sure that all the celebrating doesn't get out of hand; fights, looting or anything that will cast a cloud over our thus far success."

We're about to hear what the president has to say; come join us."

Governor Simmons asked that all incoming telephones be held and cell phones turned off and for Gene Todd to insure that everyone had access to a television set. As the clock moved toward three p.m., the television networks broke into normal programming to announce a "special emergency speech" by the President of the United States from Camp David.

Promptly at three o'clock the TV cameras centered in on the president sitting behind a desk. With seeming unfettered self confidence, he began:

"Good afternoon; I apologize for intruding into your quiet weekend, but it is imperative that I inform each of you watching on television, monitoring the internet, or listening on your radios that we are in the midst of an unseemly emergency within our great nation. No, we have not been attacked, so do not be alarmed about your safety or that of your families. All is safe within the country with the possible exception of those in the state of Texas. Earlier this morning, the great state of Texas was invaded from within--invaded by a group of traitorous individuals led by a governor, who by all accounts of his words and actions is the leader of this treacherous band. His provocative announcement this morning, pronouncing that Texas is seceding from the United States of America comes as a grievous shock to me and no doubt to each of you. But first let me assure you and especially the loyal citizens of Texas, this act of treason by the governor and a few apparently willing zealous accomplices will not stand."

The governor watched and listened to every word and nuance; several of the others glanced at one another from time to time, without speaking. The president continued.

"I will be brief; the governor of Texas has violated the constitution of the United States and that of his own state by this heinous and unpardonable act. And I want to reach out to every citizen of Texas and our great nation to ask for your support in restoring sanity and order to this astonishing provocation. At this time in our nation and the world, we cannot afford to be distracted by such an unlawful act--one that can be devastating in destroying unity and economic well-being for all our people; especially the people in the great state of Texas. The agenda before America is great and it requires the full attention and support of all of us to insure its success in changing our country to the direction we have set. That is why and for the purpose you elected me your president and I will not permit such a heinous crime such as that perpetrated by the maverick governor of one of our most cherished states and people to attempt to take law and order into his own hands and liberty away from its citizens. I have had the secretary of state contact him this morning only to be rebuffed. I also have directed the attorney general to initiate necessary legal actions to terminate this madness before it goes farther. Lastly, I hope to quell this insanity quietly, address the apparent crime that has been committed and restore law and order in the great Lone Star State promptly. Thank you."

The governor and the others in the room sat quietly for a moment reflecting on the president's words. Lt. Governor Dan Stauffer sat stone quiet in the corner as he had most of the day since he arrived that morning. He was no doubt in considerable angst; having not heard from Jacque and wondering what had happened to her. Governor Simmons looked about briefly and then back to the television screen which was flashing re-runs of the president, and finally uttered in a low voice.

"Mr. President, you and your go-along congress are the traitors and betrayers of your own office and this country. It is you who got yourself catapulted into the office of the presidency on a red carpet of smoke-filled promises, false hopes and 'change that we in Texas cannot believe in'. Mr. President, it is you who has brought this nation to the brink of a national security disaster and loss of international respect. Never in history has any president or perhaps has any world leader inflicted more damage to the economic and social policies of a country than you! Okay, folks, I got a little carried away; sorry."

He took a deep breath and looked about the room. "Well, my friends, he has spoken," he continued with a shallow exhale. "Here we are; too late to back out now unless any of you have changed your mind or position."

There was a rumble of "Never" and "No way, Governor" throughout the room.

"Della, let's get started on the confirmation process as soon as possible," Simmons said. "You set the agenda and the schedule for officially positioning me within the government of the Republic, provide me a proposed list of position leader names for vice president, attorney general, secretary of state, chief justice, secretary of defense and each of the other initial cabinet offices. I know you have already thought most of the requirements through; when do we kick it off?"

"Sir, I am virtually prepared and ready," Della replied. "I have been short-handed without the services of Jacque. I was hoping she would be back by now. (A wry smile crossed her lips). Governor, I propose that we swear you in at eleven a.m. on Monday in the auditorium of the capitol building. And, I suggest that you be sworn in by Manny. I essentially have the documents prepared and as you and I have briefly discussed, I have a list of proposed key positions for you to consider."

"Good, Della," Simmons replied with a nod; "on top of your game as always. Now, back to the president's remarks; there's no telling what they have in mind, or at this point know how to respond to our shocker. Regret we disturbed his peaceful Camp David weekend," he smirked. "It was either there, Hawaii, Cape Cod, at one of the national parks, at dinner in New York, Air Force One jetting to some other faraway place; in any event, we have his attention. Wouldn't it be great if some of our sister states would act accordingly?" He paused. "Perhaps we didn't think it all through; we may very well have co-opted several others to join us in this quest? That would have really turned the tide." He paused and sighed. "Oh well, it's us all alone here, at least for the time being. Okay, Della, you have your work to do; thank you all again and again for joining in this world-shattering event. Keep me posted on all ongoing activities within and outside the state, 'er republic! Call me day or night with any and all details; any questions or comments?"

Most of the members shook their heads without speaking and began to move back to their positions in the Command Center.

"Dan," the governor spoke; looking in the direction of Dan Stauffer. "Could I see you in my office, please; Della and Manny would you also join us."

"Take a seat please; all of you," Simmons began. "Oh, Coffee, anyone?" he asked. No one responded and sat down. "Dan," he began, "it grieves me to have this conversation; perhaps the worst of any I have ever had with a professional colleague."

Stauffer was seated upright and stolid in his chair. He did not respond.

"Mr. Stauffer," Simmons continued. "We have been on to yours and

Ms. Adams' game for quite a while. I am sure you are surprised that you haven't heard from her; that's because she has been quietly held in custody in Houston for the past few days. I am not going to admonish, curse you, or otherwise take any actions against either of you; at least for the time being or unless you force me to. I suggest strongly that the two of you quietly disappear in your own chosen directions and that we do not hear from you ever again in Texas. That's it. Do you have anything you wish to say?"

Dan Stauffer did not move; he continued to sit stiffly upright in his chair, his head slightly bowed. All eyes were on him. Finally, he stood, appearing somewhat shaky, and walked quietly out of the room. The once self-assured, bright young master of himself and others he could control had met a shocking defeat.

The weekend began to pass with relative quiet in Austin in spite of the dramatic pronouncement by the governor. There were reports of small sporadic gatherings; most were positive toward the governor's announcement while others were in mild protest which the police had to control. The same was true throughout the various communities in the state; now to be the Republic of Texas. The same was not true throughout the media world; every network and cable television channel was abuzz 24/7 with the news about the secession taking place in Texas, the president's condemnation and any other sidebars that could be factually gathered or made up. Gene Todd was occupied full-time trying to keep up with both factual events and rumors. President to be Simmons continued to take and return calls from around the country; most were supportive, encouraging and congratulatory for his bold move to affront the growing oppression by the president, his administration and the congress. Chris Mitchell kept him apprised of activities around the state; most of which were in normal modes. The military installations were being closely monitored for any unusual activity, air and vehicle traffic from a distance by DPS, rangers and the guard elements posted nearby. Zach Hollis was monitoring the FBI offices around the new Republic for the same unusual activity as he was interstate highway traffic. Making the announcement on the weekend no doubt considerably eased particular overt reactions by all agencies.

Bill Simmons was cognizant of course that the worst was yet to come. It would be months, perhaps years, before the situation settled; if ever!

Della Murphy remained busy putting final details together for the inauguration to take place on Monday morning. Many details had to be worked out, special invitations, security, media releases, etc. She was also working diligently to provide Simmons with a consideration list of prospective key positions for his administration. That chore proved the most difficult; Dan Stauffer's defection had compounded the situation, although 'no loss' in her own way of judging.

"Who can I propose for the interim vice president?" she thought to herself..."Manny Estrada, Alex Mason, General Mitchell, Zach Hollis, General Lawhorn? Each one is exceptionally bright and thoughtful, highly mature, experienced, logical thinkers, loyal and committed. What about 'me'? I fit all those criteria."

She continued to brainstorm the various positions that required to be initially filled and then she concluded the structure would be filled from the top down by the principals appointed. She would have her list completed by Sunday afternoon and provide it to Simmons for his overnight review and consideration. She would name 'herself' as the nominee for vice president.

Chapter Fourteen

Sunday began as an uneventful day with the exception of the nonstop television news coverage. Bill Simmons could not rest or relax. He had much more on his mind than he felt he could sort out in an orderly structured manner; there were a multitude of considerations, but most how to respond and react to Washington! He by and large ignored the torrent of television program coverage keeping the set on mute except for periodic peeks. The real cascading landslide was sure to come from Washington sooner or later, but in what form or nature? He could not underestimate the building of wrath back there and how it would be meted out.

"The worst is by far yet to come," he mused as he tried to focus on a list of set priorities. The impact of his and his followers' actions was settling heavy over him. "Am I up to this? Am I capable of keeping it all together and seeing it through? Will Texans accept me as their new president?" The persistent questions ran in and out of his thoughts as he tried to concentrate.

The governor's mansion outside had taken on the appearance of a fortress. The grounds were encircled with police and military vehicles; armed patrols were present at both inner and outer perimeters. The capitol building was also placed under extreme security and surveillance. Simmons did not like the appearances, but he knew for the safety and security of all concerned, it required what Chris Mitchell had planned and directed.

Della delivered her well-planned and laid-out agenda and program for the inauguration in the afternoon. It was very concise and brief to the point of hurriedly getting the necessary protocols completed, minimize the public exposure and to not gloat over the extraordinary world shattering event. Simmons pondered her every detail. She also provided him with her proposed list of administration and cabinet officials. He smiled and glanced up at her as he noted the first nominee on the list; that for vice president, but did not comment as he perused the remainder of the positions and names.

"Thank you, Della," he smiled nodding. "As usual, you have hit another home run with all of this. I don't want to comment or discuss any of it right now; I will sleep on it, if I sleep at all tonight, and we will discuss first thing in the morning and before the inauguration event. Okay?"

"Fine, sir," Della replied quietly; obviously disappointed that he did not respond with any comments on any of her suggestions. "You get some rest, 'Mr. President', and I will be available at your calling this evening or in the morning."

"Thank you, Della," he smiled. "As usual, you continue to provide life's blood to your work. God bless."

After Della departed, Simmons perused her administration and cabinet appointment suggestions. He mulled over each position, proposed individual and their particular 'fit' within the organization. "Della would make an excellent vice president of the Republic," he mused. "But, I really believe she can be much more proactive as attorney general of the Republic. This will disappoint her, but the VP, at least for now, needs to be someone less challenging and more conciliatory to be at my side and in my absence. Ah, Manny Estrada," he nodded to himself and penciled in his name as vice president.

"Della can become the AG for the Republic; she has a good legal mind and is undaunted by lawyers," he continued cogitating to himself. "I'll appoint Gene Todd as my chief of staff; he has been a life savior throughout out this process and deserves a reward. Alex Mason, secretary of state; Chris Mitchell, secretary of defense; Tom Lawhorn, chief of staff of the armed forces of Texas;" he was interrupted by the telephone.

∞

"Ms. Adams, I'm Trooper Caitlyn Rose," the female DPS officer called softly as she approached the detention cell. Following close behind her was a man dressed in a dark suit and the jail matron. It was early Sunday morning.

Jacque Adams did not look up or respond; she sat stolid, her back to the cell door, her arms wrapped around her as if she was chilled.

"Ma'am, I am here with Doctor Jacob; we are required to give you brief physical health check before you can leave," Trooper Rose continued. Jacque did not move or respond.

"I have your personal effects and luggage gathered together for you, Ma'am; if you will please come with us," the trooper beckoned as she nodded for the matron to open the cell door.

Jacque finally turned, remained seated and stared blankly at the trooper for a full minute. She was sullen; the trooper did not urge her further and stood patiently by with the matron at her side. The physician remained outside the cell. Jacque finally and mechanically rose to her feet without speaking and walked unhurriedly out of the cell with her head down and followed Trooper Rose and the physician with the matron trailing behind. They escorted her into a small office and the trooper asked her to be seated. The trooper again introduced Doctor Jacob and explained that he was going to ask her a few questions as a part of the separation process.

Without verbally responding, Jacque eased herself into one of the chairs. Doctor Jacob then introduced his nurse attendant, "Ms. Adams, this is Summer Lee; she will be assisting me as we ask you a few questions about how you are feeling."

Jacque did not respond; she sat staring at the wall. Dr. Jacob asked Trooper Rose and the jail matron to please leave them alone. "We'll be just fine," he said.

After a half hour or so, Dr. Jacob opened the door and stepped out to visit with the trooper. "She is in a deep state of depression," he said with a sigh. "She is fully cognizant of her surroundings; where she is and so on, but she isn't responsive to questions. Now that could be an act on her part or she could actually be in a subconscious state. I doubt the latter; I believe she is doing this for our benefit."

"Well, what shall we do with her, Doctor?" Trooper Rose asked.

Dr. Jacob sighed, "I'm not sure; we could hospitalize her for observation, leave here for another day or let her go. I don't recommend leaving her here in a jail cell, however; that would only add to her depression."

The door to the office where the nurse and Jacque were waiting suddenly opened and Nurse Summer Lee stepped out with Jacque right behind her. "Doctor," the nurse smiled. "Ms. Adams seems to be in full recovery! She is fully cognizant and energized."

Doctor Jacob took Jacque by the hand and she smiled at him in return. He looked into her eyes and again she gave him a big smile and said, "Doctor, I'm fine; I just had a little relapse, but all is well...I want to go home."

The doctor looked at Trooper Rose, shrugged, "Well, there's your story; these reactions are quite common when someone has undergone mild shock they become disoriented when placed in a jail cell or some other strange environment. So, I believe she should be free to go."

"You're the doctor," Trooper Rose smiled, relieved to get the issue back on schedule. "Thank you, Doctor; we appreciate your time and attention."

The trooper turned to Jacque, "Okay, Ms. Adams, it looks like you are free to go; we will need to complete a bit of paper work and you can be on your way."

They proceeded to the departure office where Jacque signed her release document. The desk officer handed over her purse and she proceeded to pick up the small roller luggage piece.

"Your car is this way, Ma'am," Trooper Rose motioned toward the door.

Jacque followed her, still somewhat sullen and robot-like without speaking. It was obvious that once out of sight of the doctor, she was still in her mind set. Her thoughts were locked on the secession announcement speech given by Bill Simmons in Austin yesterday. The reality that Texas had seceded from the U.S. was almost too much for her to bear. She and Dan Stauffer had failed and Simmons had won. What can now be done was a continuing question hammering her confused and depressed thoughts as she plodded along behind staring straight ahead without speaking.

As they arrived at her vehicle parked in the underground garage, the trooper placed the luggage piece in the rear seat and asked if she needed any assistance or directions."

"No!" Jacque replied in a subdued, but gritty voice and got into her car.

"Be safe, Ma'am," the trooper said, smiling.

Jacque started the engine and drove slowly and deliberately out of the police parking garage and onto the bright sunshiny busy Houston city street. At first she was not sure where she was and then caught a street sign. She headed west, weaving in and out of traffic toward Buffalo Drive and onto the 610 Belt Way and Highway 290 leading to Austin. She noted that they had filled her gas tank. As her head cleared and the dazed experience of the past few days began to wear off, her thoughts began to move rapidly. She reached in her purse for her cell phone, looked at it momentarily and flung it to the floor board.

"Bastards!" she whispered out loud. "They have that number tapped."

Once on Highway 290, she spotted a Wal-Mart store ahead and pulled in. She bought two "throw away" cell phones, some bottled water and got back onto the highway toward Austin.

Her first thought was to call her husband and let him know she was headed back to Austin; they had allowed her to speak to him when she was first detained and placed in the Houston police detention center. So as to not alarm him, she told him she was on official AG business. She then quickly looked up Dan Stauffer's cell number knowing full well that his phone was likely bugged; how else could they have detected their activities? She called anyway, but no answer; then she tried his home phone and again, no response. She didn't leave a message with either call and tossed the phone onto the floor mat with the other. She figured that they would likely be tracing her calls and would keep the additional "throw away" cell phone for later use. She turned on the radio and proceeded to listen to the blitz of news reporting the governor's bold pronouncement. She moved from station to station; listening to various versions of the event and commentary about what would or could happen next; reactions were coming from around the state, the country and the world. "Dramatic history was in the making," most concluded.

"Damn bastards!" she proclaimed loudly over and over. "This will not stand as they have so cleverly planned!" Her thoughts were awash with emotion and a jumble of notions. She finally began to tremble and shake so violently that she had to pull onto an access road stopped the car and burst into convulsive tears. Back in control of her nerves, she drank some water daubed her face and headed back to the highway.

❧

Meanwhile, back in Austin; "Simmons," he responded to the ring of his hot line phone. He had just enjoyed a glass of wine and his nerves were much calmer from the afternoon of reading, reviewing and reflecting on all that lay ahead. The clock on his desk showed six p.m.

"Sir, Gene here," Gene Todd replied. "Governor, 'er Mr. President, the President of the United States wishes to speak with you at about six thirty our time; twenty-five minutes or so from now. The operator will place the call on this phone if that is satisfactory with you?"

"Hmmmmm, that's interesting, any other details relative to his purpose or intent?" Simmons asked.

"No, sir, nothing else," Gene replied. "I wish I could provide you more information. Is there anything I can do at this time?"

"I would like to have you here when the call comes in, Gene," Simmons responded. "Also please contact Della and ask that she come over as well. I doubt that she can be here by the time the call comes in, but ask her to come as soon as she can."

"Yes, sir, will do and I'll be right over myself," Gene Todd replied.

"Wow!" he exhaled. "This will be a test!" He began to collect his thoughts. "Just listen," he whispered to himself. "Let him do the talking, make his pitch or proposition, remain cool and respectful."

Gene Todd entered the mansion office. "Sir, anything you want me to do to prepare?" Gene asked almost breathless from his sprint over from the capitol building.

"Yes, have a pen and pad ready and pick up the receiver of the monitor phone when I answer," Simmons replied. "Make notes as we go along; both my comments and his. At first, I wasn't going to turn on the recorder, but we will. They may have a recorder detector on their end, but what th' heck, if they call us on it, we'll turn it off."

The hot line phone rang promptly at six thirty. Bill Simmons picked up the receiver. "This is Simmons, Mr. President," Simmons responded.

"Governor Simmons, this is the chief of staff, the president will

134

be with you momentarily," the voice on the other end sternly replied. "Governor, for purposes of accuracy and if you have the capability, you may wish to record the conversation with the president. One moment, please and the president will be with you."

Bill Simmons nodded and winked at Gene Todd.

"Governor Simmons, Bill, how are you?" the President of the United States greeted. "Bill, we have not had the opportunity to meet and I regret the circumstances of this first conversation."

"Good evening, Mr. President," Simmons responded.

"Bill," the president continued quickly, an apparent sense of urgency in his voice. "I must say you have turned the nation and your great state upside down. We have no clear idea what provoked this extraordinary and for that matter wholly unlawful and illegal act of attempted desertion from the family of the United States. Let me be clear, governor, your unilateral act will not be tolerated, or accepted by me or the people of the United States."

The president quickly shifted to a soft and calmer tone. "Although you have violated the constitution of the United States, a criminal act in itself, I want to put that aside and work with you...head of state to head of state and as intelligent, rational men."

"Mr. President," Bill Simmons interjected.

"No, wait, please let me complete my remarks before you speak," the president admonished.

"Yes, sir," Simmons replied.

"Governor Simmons," the president continued. "Before you precipitate any further actions to intensify this hysteria in our country and especially within Texas, I want to pursue a course of action to stem any further damage. Your act is causing great consternation within the United States and among our allies, and we must seek a quick remedy that returns your great state and people back to normalcy and we can work together on a positive course for the future. Now, what I wish to do is send my chief of staff and a few constitutional attorneys to visit with you; I ask you and your trusted staff members to meet with them in confidence and let's work our way out of this. You have my word that if you cooperate and we can agree to a prompt solution to restore order in Texas, there will be no retribution. Do you agree to the first step?"

Simmons did not immediately respond; he glanced over at Gene

Todd just as Della Murphy entered the room. "Mr. President," he replied finally. "The actions I have taken here in Texas to sustain and maintain liberty and freedoms within Texas were not hastily made nor were they without much soul searching and anguish; I..." and he was promptly interrupted by the president.

"Governor, I neither have the time nor the patience to debate with you on the telephone," the president admonished in a cutting voice. "I am offering you an opportunity to participate in a process of recovery for your state and your people; I will work with you personally as soon as we agree to the protocols, and I assure you that when logical order can be restored, there will be no reprisals toward you or any of your people if you will just agree to take the first step in reconciliation. Do you agree?"

Bill Simmons took a deep breath and looked at Della for a reaction. She had been listening through a pair of headphones and perhaps for the first time even she was at loss for a prompt response. She stared back at him and shook her head with a stern, mouthed No! The gravity of the President of the United States on the phone personally challenging their act of secession closed in on all of all three of them in the room.

"Mr. President, thank you for your call and your concern," Simmons responded, "but we are on a course of action and journey for all Texans and we are determined to proceed. Goodnight, sir."

He looked around at Della and Gene. "Well, folks, we are either dead or alive; batten down the hatches! We have just brought the whole United States government down on our heads." He paused for a reflective moment, "Let's have a toast; Gene, you pour."

After a few minutes of reflection, he looked at Della, "Well Madam AG, let's proceed with plan A tomorrow; formally gong me as the President of the Republic of Texas as scheduled."

Jacque Adams finally made her way to her apartment; it was late... around three Sunday afternoon. Her husband greeted her warmly and began to pursue dozen of questions. She put him off with, "Please, let's go over it this evening; I am too tired to think right now."

He neither knew or suspected all that she had been up to with the Stauffer sabotage caper. That evening she laid out a long and descriptive tall tale about how she and the AG had orchestrated the secession plan for the governor and that she had been in Houston tying up loose ends before the announcement. He bought her story. She then began to put her own new plan together; she would not try to make contact with Dan Stauffer. "He has likely high-tailed it out of the country by now," she rationalized as her angry grew. She knew that her public career was now over.

She arose early on Monday morning telling her husband she had much work to do for Della. She knew that Simmons was scheduled to be inaugurated around eleven o'clock that morning. The evening before, she had tucked away a blonde wig and a pair of gloves in her briefcase, secured her husband's loaded .38 caliber service revolver from its place in the dresser drawer, and placed it in her purse. Once out of the apartment building she stopped off for a Starbuck's, began to scope out her overnight thoughts, scanned the news accounts and listened to the buzz of conversation around her. She then drove around the capitol grounds observing the flurry of activity finally parking on a shady side street off Congress Avenue. She put the blonde wig on over her short dark hair, donned a large pair of sunglasses, got out of the car and headed up the street toward the capitol building. She was familiar with all the entries and exits and had a pass key to one of them.

Once inside the building she made her way casually to the upper level above to the auditorium and where the inauguration would take place. She was familiar with a small corner office with two small windows facing down on the lower portico where chairs, tables and a lectern had been set up. She tested one of the windows to insure she could easily push it open and then pulled it back without locking it. There was an antique stand alone cloak closet which she checked out and insured that she could slip inside later if necessary and wait for the inaugural event to take place. She had a couple of hours before it was scheduled to begin, so she moved back down to the main floor picked up a newspaper and strolled casually into the coffee shop where she waited observing and listening to the exciting chatter about the ongoing events. At ten thirty she walked back upstairs observing that there was surprisingly very little increased security within the building; it was all concentrated outside.

"Highly confident, aren't they!" she thought to herself. She reentered the small office, locked the door from the inside and prepared the cloak closet should she have to scamper into it if someone checked out the office. Her feelings ranged from anger, fear, to apprehension and depression; she had not even considered how she would or even could escape after she completes the deed she had hastily planned.

At eleven a.m. sharp, the "Eyes of Texas" began to pipe loudly over the large speakers set up for the occasion. No one had attempted to check out her sequestered location. She peered through the window down to those seated behind the lectern. She had a clear un-obstructive view only about fifteen yards from Simmons who was seated between his wife and Attorney General Della Murphy. On Della's right side sat Manny Estrada and Alex Mason; other group members were in the Command Center. Jacque Adams was surprised at her calmness. The anger and vengeance so weld up within her over the last several days had now become intoxicated with cold revenge.

"There's no need to wait any longer," she thought to herself; took in a deep breath and removed the revolver from her purse. She carefully pulled back the hammer and held the pistol securely in her gloved right hand. The music over the loudspeakers was ear-shattering. She opened and peered through the window and lined up the sights to the top back of Bill Simmons head. It had been several years since she last fired a weapon on her father's ranch, but she felt confident as she aimed at her target.

She fired the revolver once killing Simmons instantly. She then quickly moved the barrel toward Della Murphy and fired again. She missed Della with the second shot. She stepped back from the window and hurriedly tossed the pistol into the closet. She then ran to the exit door partially opening it and saw two capitol policemen rushing down the hall to where the gunfire came. Jacque quickly closed the door and rushed into the closet and closed the door. With their weapons in hand, the two policemen entered the room and looked around not seeing anything or anyone.

"Better check the closet," one of them said. As the policeman walked across the floor to open the closet, Jacque picked up the revolver and placed it next to her temple and pulled the trigger; blood and tissue splattered in all directions. Hearing the gunshot the policemen instantly hesitated, cocked their weapons, waited a moment, and then one slowly opened the door. His eyes focused on the bloody scene and then to the body on the closet floor. The officer stooped down, checked for some sign of life, but found none. Jacque Adams was dead.

Both Simmons and Jacque Adams' bodies were removed and taken by ambulance to University Hospital. There was no reason to perform an autopsy as it could not be clearer as to the cause of their deaths.

———— Chapter Fifteen ————

The shock of Governor Bill Simmons' assassination once again rocked the state and the nation. Jacque Adams was identified as the assassin with many conservatives and traditionalists asking why she would do such a horrible act to the incoming President of the Texas Republic. Others seem to accept that this was often the fate of those charismatic leaders who try to bring about change.

During the next several days, the death of Bill Simmons remained the hottest news item and was covered by local, national and international media. While a few Texans and other outsiders did not approve of Simmons' move to secede they never thought that an insider would be the one who would kill him; there were other ways to remove Simmons was the recurring comments made by anchors, callers, and bloggers.

With the death of Simmons, Della Murphy stepped forward to take charge of the state of affairs. Dan Stauffer had left the state and would play no role in the upcoming transition. Tuesday morning, she summoned and held consultations with all the members and played the recording of the conversation between the president and Bill Simmons. She called for a vote of confidence to continue with the secession now in progress, "In the name of a Texas patriot, President-elect William Simmons, we can do this!" she loudly voiced.

The vote failed. Most of the members now felt that the overwhelming trauma of Simmons' death was more than they could take with the ominous thoughts that even more violence could come notwithstanding the weight of the U.S. government cascading down upon them. They would seek asylum and absolution from the president, extract what concessions they might and put Texas back into statehood.

"With our vote to acquiesce, let us all be prepared to meet and work with the delegation the U.S. President will be sending to Austin. I will call them right away to let them know our decision. God bless Texas!" Della declared, greatly disappointed.

Della, Manny, Alex, Generals Mitchell and Lawhorn arrived at the capitol building at nine o'clock Wednesday morning. They would spend the day with the Washington group who were arriving in Austin later on that morning. During their conversations, it was notable that there were no investigative questions being put to them; rather the main concerned of group of four from Washington was mostly procedural with questions like "how do we do this in order to fit within the constitutional requirements of both Texas and the U.S.?" Della and her cohorts felt the president was keeping his word regarding amnesty. While on lunch break, Della mentioned that maybe the FBI would be the ones who would be seeking evidence against the so-called radical Texans involved in the secession conspiracy and they would take their time, acting when things cooled down. It was known that depending on its chief, the FBI often acted on their own regardless of presidential directives. The fact that Simmons was dead took a little spunk out of the blame game. Also there was not a call by any groups or news media to go after the others who started the trouble. Bill Simmons, the leader, was dead; his killer was also dead—enough is enough!

Della knew that in some respects most people just wanted to get on with returning to statehood some believing that the entire ruckus was a ruse just to get Washington's attention. If they only knew, like she did, that the act to secede was firmly embedded in the mind, heart, and soul of Bill Simmons who inspired her and others to feel the same; no, it was not a ruse. Della knew it was a mission designed to fully magnify the magnificence of Texans setting them apart from all others to glorify in their special history and their right to self-determination. She also believed this sense of thinking and feeling would not go away with the death of Bill Simmons.

Thursday morning at ten o'clock Della and her team were asked to sit in on a debriefing by the Washington group. They had concluded their review and felt that their presence was no longer needed. There were some administrative actions that needed to be done to facilitate the move back to statehood including appointing a new governor which the people of Texas could decide. Again, no mention was made of any investigative actions directed toward the people who participated in the secession. The group seemed eager to leave Austin and return to their home base. None had a favorable comment to make about Texas, its people, food, or way of life. To them, Texas was a foreign country. They all shook hands with a final exchange of pleasantries and the meeting ended.

As Della and her 'Texans' left the room she reminded them of the memorial for Bill Simmons in the rotunda at three o'clock. Alex and Manny would be attending, breaking away from their legislature business of trying to get a potential name of a legislator to become the new governor to be agreed upon and voted for by both houses. Manny privately mentioned to Della that only two junior legislators showed any interest in the job. Manny said there was a move by some minority legislative groups to draft Alex, but Alex was hesitant to take on the challenge especially when thinking of his role in the secession. Della understood, but knew instantly there would be a benefit to the legacy of Bill Simmons if Alex or Manny were to become governor. Her last words to Manny "Do your best to elect Alex, if not, I urge you to take on this responsibility."

Della, General Mitchell and General Lawhorn had a few minutes to spare before attending the memorial so they stopped for a glass of ice tea in the cafeteria. Tom Lawhorn opened the conversation: "My head has not stopped turning since I first heard of Bill Simmons' death. The thought of Jacque being an assassin never occurred to me. It is almost overbearing. Furthermore, not knowing just what ultimately the feds will do regarding our complicity only adds to the problem. I mean, can we trust the president's statements and will he stick with them even though he will be condemned by the left for not hanging us. I am just about burned out."

General Mitchell responded, "Tom, hang in there for a few more days and we should know something. I have been thinking about what their options might be and I now believe the antagonists will drag their feet for some time and then find a way to go along with the president. It would make sense that that they wouldn't want our prosecution to be a match to start another fire for secession by a new group. Remember, the TEA and TAG groups are still active and probably won't go away anytime soon. They were in our camp and would raise holy hell if we were subjected to a public trial, at least I would hope so."

"Chris, you have a good way of assessing situations and in this one I tend to agree with you. I, too, think the feds will go along with the president and will quietly let go of the secession issue." Tom replied. "Too, I haven't heard any rumors from my friends in the Pentagon."

Della, still subdued, spoke; "Let's hope that both of you are right in your judgment of our status. As soon as the new governor takes over, I will be leaving government and, if I am not disbarred, I will return to private practice never again will I consider the world of politics. It just wouldn't be the same without Simmons."

Chris responded, "My initial plan is to return to my neighborhood and do some writing, maybe about what we all tried to do but failed."

Tom, who seemed rather tired with his head drooping down looking at his empty glass added, "As soon as I can I am heading home, plant a garden and try to enjoy my retirement. I agree with Della that in my lifetime there will never be another Bill Simmons. His loss is the hurt that I feel most."

"It's time to go," Della said rather abruptly.

Arriving at the rotunda, Della, Chris and Tom went directly to Mrs. Bill Simmons and the family offering their sympathies and condolences.

"He was a great, compassionate, and dedicated leader who I will terribly miss," Della said to Mrs. Simmons, gently hugging her.

Manny and Alex stood nearby with several other legislators. After reviewing the remains of Simmons appropriately placed in a silver plated casket, they all gathered in the open section of the rotunda.

"I wish to thank each and every one of you for coming to this gathering," Mrs. Simmons began. "Your presence helps to lighten the heavy load and sorrow we feel in our hearts. I have asked Representative Alex Mason to lead us in prayer, after which, Attorney General Della Murphy will share her feelings."

Alex Mason stepped forward, nodding to the assemblage. "My words to you will be taken from a poem that I wrote last night while reflecting on our loss of this great man. I have titled it: *An Ode to William Simmons*. On this solemn occasion I believe it expresses our feelings for our fallen friend; let's bow our heads."

"You've gone first leaving us so much alone.
We'll have to be content with happy days we've known.
This spring will surely bring more bonnets blue,
and in early fall when live oak leaves fall we'll think of you.

You've gone first while we stay for battles to be fought.
The pride and honor you taught us will be our deepest thought.
We'll often think of you as we smile through falling tears.
Your memory will carry us onward through the coming years.

You've gone first leaving a pathway for our dignity and hope.
Look down from Heaven and help us as we try to cope.
Existing without you now seems forlorn with painful regrets
as you dwell in paradise watching our beautiful Texas sunsets.

You've gone first and left your dream of Texans freedom's joy.
The memory of you is one thing that death will not destroy.
Our weeping sad eyes gaze upward waiting for your nod
to have Texas a free nation under the principles of God."

Alex concluded his prayer remarks and stepped back with the others and Della moved forward. With moist eyes, Della sighed deeply and looked at the Simmons' family. "Today," she began, "we are shedding tears for a man who understood the aspirations of Texans much more than we do ourselves. Alex's chosen words have made us even sadder about our losing the promise of freedom for all Texans.

"The leadership qualities Bill Simmons demonstrated are rarely found in today's political environment. Having served in combat in Vietnam, he had a special place in his heart for all veterans.

"The Simmons family," she continued, "have told me that President Simmons, yes, for those of us who believed and followed him, he was the President of the Republic of Texas when he was assassinated and that is what his gravestone will read. Mrs. Simmons has informed me that he requested upon his death that his ashes be spread over the great state of Texas. Let me tell all Texas patriots that after his ashes cover our fertile soil, the flowers at the Alamo and the bluebonnets that grow on our Texas grave yards and highways will be a bit bluer and brighter this year because of what he tried to do and that was to restore the pride and glory of the Republic of Texas so rightly earned over our special history from the blood, sweat, and tears of our native sons and daughters.

"In losing his life to a murderous assassin, he rekindled the spirit and pride of a once proud nation: the Republic of Texas. There are times in one's life when a higher goal must be pursued. Our departed and beloved President believed that having Texas independent under the principles of God was one of those times. For a bit of time he gave us our independence and the eyes of Texas shined in the glow of freedom just like in the spring of 1836.

"President Simmons' dreams will live on remaining in the hearts and minds of Texans who still yearn for independence. There are active groups out there who will continue to find ways to defy the liberal impositions that no doubt will continue to come from Washington. Maybe one day a Texas patriot in the mold of President Simmons will finish the job once and forever. Heaven is surely excited that such a noble person arrived there early; but for the Simmons family and those of us who loved and admired this man it is a feeling of deep sorrow and loss. Those who were close to him knew that his heart was as big as Texas, possessing a soft tenderness that most of us are incapable of demonstrating. The spot President Simmons occupied in our hearts and minds will live on forever in a special place in Heaven. That he tried to give us our freedom, that's all we need to know about this great man.

"In this time of sorrow we weep for the man who inspired us to seek dreams of independence and freedom, I ask you to remember our pursuit and these past few days as you would remember the Alamo. I also ask you to remember President Simmons as you would Colonel Travis, Davy Crockett and Jim Bowie as they too died trying to give freedom to the Republic of Texas. May God bless each of you, the United States of America, and God bless Texas."

Della concluded with a forced smile and walked over to the Simmons family hugging each. After leaving the rotunda, she met briefly with Chris Mitchell, Tom Lawhorn, Manny and Alex saying, "I suppose the only thing we can do now is just let things play out. Manny you and Alex will have much work to do in the legislative arena. If I can assist you please contact me. Chris, Tom, perhaps this is the time to say goodbye to you knowing you are finally heading home for good. Thank all of you for your service to our country and to Texas. I shall never forget you and your willingness to sacrifice all for our noble cause. After shaking the hands of her team and then softly saying goodbye she turned and walked away. After sharing a few remarks with each other the rest bid farewell and departed the capitol grounds wearing a smile and feeling rather accomplished.

Epilogue

The great experiment was now at an end. Few could have predicted the tragic outcome. Envy, greed and zealous pursuit of position and power frequently create enemies within. Governor Bill Simmons' loyalty and devotion to the people of his proud state of Texas was historical and unrivaled. Simmons, like Sam Houston and Stephen F. Austin, with pure character and noble intentions had sought to lead his people out of the wilderness of growing socialism and diminishing moral standards that was threatening the traditions of Texans and because of this revolutionary spirit he was assassinated. He is now honored by all freedom loving Texans who will always hold his name in deep reverence. Others who were faithless to his cause are left with broken lives and tarnished names; they would likewise be despised by all real Texans for their acts of betrayal.

The President of the United States ordered all flags, state and national, to be lowered to half staff and to remain so for thirty days in honor of the military service and patriotism of Governor Bill Simmons of Texas. Some commented that this was done to gain support of those Texans who supported the wishes and aspirations of Governor Simmons. Some thought it as just a way to get closure on a ticklish political situation.

~

The traumatic events in Texas had a sobering effect on the U.S. President. He immediately called for his advisors and the congress to review some of the more radical programs which he, himself, had brought forth and he reminded them of the 10th Amendment. Although Governor Bill Simmons had sacrificed his life for his belief in his state and his people it had not been entirely in vain. He had impacted the whole of the United States government. Many governors and legislators were now empowered ready and willing to challenge the president and congress on programs that suggested a greater role for central government or a loss of power for the individual states. Texas and some southern states began to staunchly promote the return of traditional values and to what America truly stands for. National security took on a new importance.

Many in Texas demanded that the U.S. government, regardless of the party in power, recognize that Texas and Texans are not like people who live in Boston, New York City, or Hollywood. Most Texans love their traditions which are grounded in their magnificent history and they are a proud and determined people who love God, family, and freedom. They are willing to fight and to die to keep their traditional way of life. Every time they think of the Alamo, Goliad and Bill Simmons, Texans know that freedom is not free.

During the first few months afterwards, there were editorial pages in several conservative Texas newspapers stating that returning to being a part of the United States will never take away the true meaning of just what it means to be a Texan. In their editorial reviews it was made clear that what Governor Simmons tried to do was in true Texas character which is rooted in Texas history. For Texans, it is the character of a person, whether in public or private life, that counts and it doesn't matter if they are in high office living in a mansion or in a shotgun shack on an east Texas farm. Character is the essence of nobility for the poor and an unwavering obligation of the wealthy and Texans understand this principle.

Some local news media went on to say that when this momentous event becomes written history it will clearly state that Texans owe a great debt of gratitude to Governor Simmons and those who bravely stepped forward to lead Texas away from the sure destruction by an oppressive national government movement. By remembering the secessionists goals and ideals, which were aimed at preserving the history and traditions of Texas, future generations will have another reason for exhibiting pride in being Texans.

In the months that followed, Texas reconstituted itself as one of the proud states within the Union. Manny Estrada was appointed interim governor and a little known senator from Tyler was chosen lieutenant governor pending a special election. Many in Texas continue to feel that the goal Simmons had for Texas was the correct one and that Texas is destined to become even more proud because of the patriotic heroism and sacrifice of the latter day "Sam Houston," Bill Simmons.

Among Simmons' followers, Della Murphy, Chris Mitchell, Tom Lawhorn, Manny Estrada, Alex Mason, Gene Todd, Zach Hollis, Gordon Giles and others who shared in Bill Simmons' dream of a better future for Texas would come to be held forever in deep admiration by many. No federal government agency would dare bring them forward to answer why they tried to free Texas by an act of secession. In their hearts they all loved America and they would now do their best to contribute to its security and prosperity. To do otherwise would be to discredit and dishonor the thousands of Texans who have served and died in past and present wars protecting America. Each would over the years continue to exhibit pride that they were part of Simmons 'freedom's dream' and they would remember it as their proudest moment. In doing so, they would not forget the journey Bill Simmons took them on and that was to have *Texas a free nation under God.*

——— Texas History Timeline ———

Important Dates, Events, and Milestones

Source: E-Reference Desk

16th Century

Early European Exploration and Settlement

Mid-1519 - Spanish explorer Alonso Alvarez de Pineda maps Texas coastline.

1528 - Alvar Núñez Cabeza de Vaca shipwrecked near Galveston begin exploration.

1541 - Francisco Vázquez de Coronado crosses the Texas Panhandle in search of the seven cities of Cibola.

1554 - Coronado dies. He is one of the first white men to explore Texas, and leader of one of 20 Spanish explorations of the area.

1598 - *April 30* - Thanksgiving is held near present-day El Paso by Juan de Oñate, the members of his expedition and natives of the region.

17th Century

1629 - Jumano Indians requested Spanish missionaries from New Mexico to travel to the vicinity of present-day San Angelo and instruct the Jumanos about Christianity.

1682 - First Spanish mission, Corpus Christi de la Isleta, is established a few miles from present-day El Paso.

1685 - *February 16* - French explorer Rene-Robert Cavelier, Sieur de La Salle, looking for the mouth of the Mississippi River, lands in Texas by mistake. He establishes a colony, Fort St. Louis, on Garcitas Creek in present-day Victoria County.

1687 - *March 19* - La Salle is killed by several of his own men at an unknown East Texas location.

1688 - *January* - Colonists at Fort St. Louis not felled by Indians, disease, poisonous snakes and malnutrition are finished off by Karankawa Indians.

1689 - *April 2* - Spanish Gen. Alonso de León's expedition finds the remains of Fort St. Louis. Fearing French intentions to lay claim to Spanish territory, the Spanish begin establishing missions and settlements in East Texas.

1690 - *May* - First East Texas mission under construction, San Francisco de los Tejas, near present-day Weches, Houston Co. The mission is closed in 1693.

18th Century

1716-1789 - Throughout the 18th Century, Spain established Catholic missions in Texas, and the towns of San Antonio, Goliad and Nacogdoches.

1716 - Spanish build a presidio, Nuestra Señora de los Dolores de los Tejas, to protect the East Texas missions.

1718 - *May 1* - San Antonio de Valero mission, known as the Alamo was the chapel, is founded in San Antonio.

1720 - *February* - San José y San Miguel de Aguayo mission founded near San Antonio de Valero.

1731 - 3 East Texas missions moved to San Antonio because of economics and named Nuestra Señora de la Purisima Concepción de Acuna, San Francisco de la Espada and San Juan Capistrano.

March 7 - 55 Canary Islanders arrive in San Antonio to establish a civilian settlement, San Fernando de Béxar.

Aug. 1 - First election held in Texas, voters choose officials of the municipal government of San Fernando.

1745 - Missions at San Antonio are producing thousands of pounds of cotton annually.

1758 - *March 16* - Santa Cruz de San Sabá mission near present-day Menard destroyed and eight residents killed by Comanches and their allies.

1759 - *August* - Spanish troops on a retaliatory raid are defeated by Indian residents of a large encampment at Spanish Fort in present-day Montague County.

1779 - Group of settlers led by Antonio Gil Ybarbo (sometimes spelled Ibarvo or Y'barvo) establishes a civilian community near an abandoned mission site; the new town is called Nacogdoches.

19th Century

1810 - *Sept. 16* - Father Miguel Hidalgo y Costillo and several hundred of his parishioners seize the prison at Dolores, Mexico, beginning Mexico's struggle for independence from Spain.

1812 - *August 8* - About 130-men strong, the Gutierrez-Magee Expedition crossed the Sabine from Louisiana in a rebel movement against Spanish rule in Texas.

1813 - Texas' first newspaper, Gaceta de Texas, founded by José Alvarez de Toledo in Nacogdoches.

Dec. 26 - Spanish government grants Moses Austin permission to establish a colony of Anglo-Americans in the Texas area. When he dies the following June, his son, Stephen F. Austin, receives authority to continue the colonizing effort.

1814 - *June* - Moses Austin dies; his son, Stephen F. Austin, receives authority to continue the colonizing effort.

1817-1820 - Jean Laffite occupied Galveston Island and used it as a base for his smuggling and privateering.

1818 - *September 12* - A hurricane wrecks the fleet of pirate Jean Lafitte in Galveston.

1821 - *Aug. 24* - Mexico gains independence from Spain.

October 13 - Jane Long gives birth to the first Anglo child born in Texas, a girl named Mary James.

1823 - *Jan. 3* - Stephen F. Austin received a grant from the Mexican government and began colonization in the region of the Brazos River. Mexican officials approve Austin's plan to bring three hundred families into his colony. This group becomes known as the "Old Three Hundred."

Mid-1824 - Constitution of 1824 gave Mexico a republican form of government. It failed to define the rights of the states within the republic, including Texas

1826 - *Dec. 21* - The Declaration of Independence of the republic of Fredonia is signed at Nacogdoches.

1827 - *January 31* - This so-called Fredonian Rebellion is an attempt by empresario Haden Edwards to separate his colony from Mexico. The rebels flee when approached by Mexican troops.

1829 - *October* - First of several large groups of Irish immigrants arrive to settle in South Texas.

1830 - *April 6* - Mexican government stops legal immigration into Texas from the United States except in special cases. Relations between Anglo settlers and the Mexican government deteriorate.

1831 - Johann Friedrich Ernst, his wife and five children are the first German family to arrive in Texas, settling in present-day Austin County.

Revolution and the Republic of Texas

1832 - *June 26* - First bloodshed of the Texas Revolution takes place at Velasco when Texans, transporting a cannon from Brazoria to Anahuac, are challenged by Mexican forces at Velasco. The Mexicans surrender on June 29.

1835 - *Oct. 2* - Mexican troops attempt to retrieve a cannon that had been given to Gonzales colonists for protection from Indian attack. The skirmish that ensues as Gonzales residents dare the Mexicans to "come and take it" is considered the opening battle of the Texas Revolution.

Oct. 10 - Gail Borden begins publishing the newspaper "Telegraph and Texas Register" at San Felipe de Austin.

Nov. 1 - A "consultation" convenes at San Felipe; on Nov. 7 the delegates agree to establish a provisional government.

Nov. 24 - The Texas Rangers organization is officially established by Texas' provisional government. Although Stephen F. Austin had hired 10 frontiersmen as "rangers" to help protect his colonists against Indian raids in 1823, not until 1835 was the law-enforcement group formally organized.

1836 - *March 2* - Texas Declaration of Independence is adopted at Washington-on-the-Brazos.

March 6 - 3-day siege of the Alamo by Mexican troops led by Gen. Antonio López de Santa Anna ends on this day with a battle in which all remaining defenders are killed.

March 10 - Sam Houston abandons Gonzales and retreats eastward to avoid the advancing Mexican army. Panicky settlers in the area flee as well in an exodus called the Runaway Scrape.

March 27 - About 350 Texan prisoners, including their commander James Fannin, are executed at Goliad by order of Santa Anna. An estimated 30 Texans escape.

April 21 - In a battle lasting 18 minutes, Texan troops led by Sam Houston defeat the Mexican army commanded by

Santa Anna at San Jacinto near present-day Houston. Houston reports that 630 Mexican troops were killed and 730 were taken prisoner. Of the Texas troops, nine of a force of 910 were killed or mortally wounded, and 30 were less seriously wounded.

May 14 - Santa Anna and Texas' provisional president David Burnet sign two Treaties of Velasco—one public, the other secret—ending the Texas Revolution. The treaties were, however, violated by both sides. Texas' independence was not recognized by Mexico and Texas' boundary was not determined until the Treaty of Guadalupe Hidalgo, which ended the Mexican War, was signed in 1848.

Sept. 5 - Voters of the new republic choose their first elected officials: Sam Houston becomes president and Lorenzo de Zavala, vice president. The voters also overwhelmingly approve a referendum requesting annexation by the United States. US President Martin Van Buren refuses to consider it, however, citing fear of war with Mexico and constitutional scruples.

Oct. - The first Congress of the Republic of Texas convenes at Columbia.

1837 - Republic of Texas is officially recognized by the United States, and later by France, England, the Netherlands and Belgium.

1839 - *Aug. 1* - First sale of town lots in the new capital of the Republic, which is named for Stephen F. Austin, is held.

1840 - *March 19* - Comanches, led by a dozen chiefs, meet with officials of Texas government to negotiate a peace treaty. Believing the Comanches to have reneged on a promise to release all white prisoners, the Texans take the chiefs prisoner. During the Council House fight that follows, 35 Comanches are killed, as are seven Texans.

Aug. 5 - Near Hallettsville, Comanches, in retaliation for the Council House Fight, begin killing and looting their way across Central Texas. Texas Rangers and a volunteer army defeat the Comanches on Aug. 11 at Plum Creek near Lockhart.

1841 - *22 May* - The Republic of Texas relied heavily on volunteers to patrol areas and in 1839 John B Denton joined and was commissioned as a Captain in Brig. General Edward Tarrant's (Tarrant County) 4th Brigade, Texas Militia. In April, 1841 a family by the name of Ripley was killed by Indians and a group of scouts lead by Captain Denton along with Henry Stout was sent out to find them. On May 22, 1841, his unit attacked the Indians of Keechi Village at Village Creek, about six miles east of the site of Fort Worth and Denton was killed. His body was brought back by horseback and he was buried in an unmarked grave on the east bank of Oliver Creek where it met a stream now called Denton Creek located in an area now called Denton County. He left behind a widow and six children. Denton, Texas is his namesake.

June 20 - The Santa Fé Expedition, launched without Texas Congressional authorization by Pres. Mirabeau B. Lamar, leaves Central Texas on its way west to establish trade with and solidify Texas' claims to territory around Santa Fé. Members of group are taken prisoner by Mexican troops, marched to Mexico City and imprisoned. They are finally released in 1842.

1842 - The first seeds of large-scale German immigration to Texas are sown when a German society, the Adelsverein, purchases land for settlements in Central Texas.

Annexation and Statehood

1845 - *February 1* - Baylor University is founded.

March 1 - US Congress passes a "Joint Resolution for Annexing Texas to the United States."

Mid-March - The first of many large groups of Germans arrive in Central Texas, settling at New Braunfels.

July 4 - The Texas Constitutional Convention votes to accept the United States annexation proposal; it drafts an Annexation Ordinance and State Constitution to submit to the voters of Texas.

Oct. 13 - Texas voters overwhelmingly approve annexation, the new state constitution and the annexation ordinance.

Dec. 29 - The US Congress approves, and President James K. Polk signs, the "Joint Resolution for the Admission of the State of Texas into the Union." Texas becomes the 28th state.

1846 - *Feb. 19* - Formal transfer of government take place until this date.

May 8 - Battle of Palo Alto near Brownsville is first major battle of the two-year Mexican War.

1848 - *Feb. 2* - Treaty of Guadalupe Hidalgo is signed, ending the War with Mexico and specifying the location of the international boundary.

1850 - *Feb. 11* - The first railroad to actually begin operation in Texas is chartered by the state government. The Buffalo Bayou, Brazos and Colorado begins operation in 1853.

Nov. 25 - Texas' governor signs the Compromise of 1850, in which Texas gives up its claim to land that includes more than half of what is now New Mexico, about a third of Colorado, a corner of Oklahoma and a small portion of Wyoming in exchange for the United States' assumption of $10 million in debt; Texas keeps its public lands.

1854 - Two reservations are established for Indians in West-Central Texas: one for Comanches on the Clear Fork of the Brazos in Throckmorton County, the other for more sedentary Indian groups, such as Tawakonis, Wacos and Tonkawas, near Fort Belknap in Young County.

1856 - *March 27* - Col. Robert E. Lee arrives in San Antonio. He serves at Camp Cooper on the Comanche reservation beginning April 9. He returns to Washington for a short time, coming back to San Antonio and Fort Mason in February 1860.

April 29 - Fifty-three camels arrive at port of Indianola for a US Army experiment using them for pack animals in the arid areas of the Southwest.

1859 - *July 13* - Violent clashes between Juan "Cheno" Cortina and Anglo lawmen begin in the Brownsville area in the Lower Rio Grande Valley. Texas Rangers and federal troops eventually halt the so-called "Cortina War" in 1875.

July - Indians on the West-Central Texas reservations are moved by the federal government to reservations in Indian Territory (now Oklahoma).

Secession and Civil War

1861 - *Feb. 1* - The Secession Convention approves an ordinance withdrawing Texas from Union; the action is ratified by the voters on Feb. 23 in a referendum vote. Secession is official on March 2.

Feb. 13 - Robert E. Lee is ordered to return to Washington from regimental headquarters at Fort Mason to assume command of the Union Army. Instead, Lee resigns his commission; he assumes command of the Confederate Army by June 1862.

March 1 - Texas accepted as a state by the provisional government of the Confederate States of America, even before its secession from the Union is official.

March 5 - The Secession Convention approves an ordinance accepting Confederate statehood.

March 16 - Sam Houston resigns as governor in protest against secession

1862 - *Aug. 10* - About 68 Union loyalists, mostly German immigrants from the area of Comfort, in Central Texas, start for Mexico in an attempt to reach US troops; 19 are killed by Confederates on the Nueces River. Eight others are killed on Oct. 18 at the Rio Grande. Others drown attempting to swim the river. Their deaths are commemorated in Comfort by the Treue der Union (True to the Union) monument.

October - Forty-two men thought to be Union sympathizers are hanged at various times during October in Gainesville.

1865 - *May 13* - The Battle of Palmito Ranch is fought near Brownsville, after the official end of the Civil War, because word of the war's end at Appomattox on April 9 has not yet reached troops in Texas.

Reconstruction to the 20th Century

1865 - *June 19* - Gen. Gordon Granger arrives at Galveston to announce that slavery has been abolished, an event commemorated today by the festival known as Juneteenth.

Sept. - The Bureau of Refugees, Freedmen and Abandoned Lands (the Freedmen's Bureau) begins operating in Texas, charged with helping former slaves make the transition to freedom.

1866 - *March 15* - The Constitutional Convention approves an ordinance to nullify the actions of the Secession Convention.

Aug. 20 - President Andrew Johnson issues a proclamation of peace between the United States and Texas.

Cattle drives, which had been occasional in the 1830s, sporadic during the 1840s and 1850s, and almost nonexistent during the Civil War, begin in earnest, mostly to markets and railheads in Midwest. They are at their peak for only about 20 years, until the proliferation of railroads makes them unnecessary.

1867-1870 - Congressional (or Military) Reconstruction replaces Presidential Reconstruction.

1869 - *Nov. 30* - Texas voters approve a new state constitution.

1870 - *March 30* - President Grant signs the act readmitting Texas to Congressional representation. Edmund J. Davis becomes the first Republican governor of Texas.

1871 - *May* - Seven men in a wagon train are massacred at Salt Creek, about 20 miles west of Jacksboro, by Kiowas and Comanches led by chiefs Satanta, Big Tree, Satank and Eagle Heart.

1872 - *Oct.* - Construction begins on the Texas & Pacific Railway; the 125-mile stretch between Longview and Dallas opens for service on July 1, 1873.

1873 - Black "Buffalo Soldiers" are first posted to Texas, eventually serving at virtually every frontier fort in West Texas from the Rio Grande to the Panhandle, as well as in other states.

Houston and Texas Central Railway reaches the Red River, connecting there with the Missouri, Kansas and Texas Railroad and creating the first all-rail route from Texas to St. Louis and the East.

1874 - *Jan. 17* - Inauguration of Democrat Richard Coke as governor marks the end of Reconstruction in Texas.

Sept. 28 - Col. Ranald Mackenzie leads the 4th US Cavalry in the Battle of Palo Duro Canyon, south of present-day Amarillo, an encounter that ends with the confinement of southern Plains Indians in reservations in Indian Territory. This makes possible the wholesale settlement of the western part of the state.

1876 - *Feb. 15* - Present state constitution is adopted.

Oct. 4 - The Agricultural and Mechanical College, later Texas A&M University, opens at College Station, becoming the first public institution of higher learning in the state.

Charles Goodnight establishes the JA Ranch in Palo Duro Canyon, the first cattle ranch located in the Panhandle.

1877 - *Sept.* - The El Paso Salt War is the culmination of a long dispute caused by Anglos' attempts to take over salt-mining rights at the foot of Guadalupe Peak, a traditionally Mexican-American salt source.

1881 - *Dec. 16* - The Texas & Pacific Railway reaches Sierra Blanca in West Texas, about 90 miles east of El Paso.

1883 - *Sept. 15* - The University of Texas classes begin.

1886 - *Aug. 19-21* - Hurricane destroys or damages every house in the port of Indianola, finishing the job started by another storm 11 years earlier. Indianola is never rebuilt.

1888 - *May 16* - Present state capitol is dedicated.

1891 - The Railroad Commission, proposed by Gov. James Hogg, is established by the Texas legislature to regulate freight rates and to establish rules for railroad operations.

1894 - *June 9* - Oil is discovered at Corsicana; a commercial field opens in 1896, becoming the first small step in Texas' rise as a major oil producer.

1898 - *May 16* - Teddy Roosevelt arrives in San Antonio to recruit and train "Rough Riders" for the First Volunteer Cavalry to fight in the Spanish-American War in Cuba.

20th Century

1900 - *Sept. 8* - The "Great Hurricane," destroys much of Galveston and kills 6,000 people.

1901 - Oil found by mining engineer Capt. A.F. Lucas at Spindletop near Beaumont catapults Texas into the petroleum age.

1902 - Poll tax becomes a requirement for voting.

1906 - Texans votes for US senator in the Democratic primary, although the Texas legislature retains ultimate appointment authority, primary voters can express their preferences.

1910 - *March 2* - Lt. Benjamin D. Foulois makes first military air flight in a Wright brothers plane at Fort Sam Houston in San Antonio.

1911-1920 - Mexican civil war spills across the border, as refugees seek safety, combatants seek each other, and Texas settlements are raided for supplies by all sides in the fighting. Pancho Villa and his followers are active along the border during some of this time.

1916 - Texas voters able to directly elect US senators.

1917-1918 - World War I.

1917 - Gov. James Ferguson is impeached and convicted; he leaves office.

1918 - *March* - Texas women win the right to vote in primary elections. Annie Webb Blanton becomes the first woman elected to a statewide office when she is elected State Superintendent of Public Instruction.

1919 - Responding to anti-German sentiment, Gov. William P. Hobby vetoes appropriations for German Dept. of The University of Texas.

1920 - Large-scale agricultural irrigation begins in the High Plains.

1925 - Miriam "Ma" Ferguson becomes Texas' first woman governor, serving as a figurehead for her husband, former Gov. James E. Ferguson.

Sept. 30 - Texas Tech University begins classes in Lubbock as Texas Technological College.

1928 - *June 26-29* - The Democratic National Convention is held in Houston, the first nominating convention held in a Southern city since 1860.

1929 - *Feb. 17* - The League of United Latin American Citizens (LULAC) is founded in Corpus Christi.

1930 - *Sept. 5* - The Daisy Bradford #3 well, drilled near Turnertown in Rusk County by wildcatter C.M. (Dad) Joiner, blows in, heralding the discovery of the huge East Texas Oil Field.

1936 - *June 6* - Texas Centennial Exposition opens at Dallas' Fair Park; it runs until Nov. 29.

1937 - *March 18* - A massive explosion, blamed on a natural-gas leak beneath the London Consolidated School building in Rusk County, kills an estimated 296 students and teachers. Subsequent deaths of people injured in the explosion bring the death count to 311. As a result, the Texas legislature requires that a malodorant be added to the odorless gas so that leaks can be more easily detected.

1941-1945 - World War II.

1943 - *June* - A race riot in Beaumont leads to a declaration of martial law.

1947 - *April 16* - The French-owned SS Grandcamp, carrying ammonium nitrate, explodes in the Texas City harbor, followed the next morning by the explosion of the SS High Flyer. The disaster kills almost 600 and injures at least 4,000 more. The concussion is felt 75 miles away in Port Arthur, and the force creates a 15-foot tidal wave.

1948 - Lyndon B. Johnson beats Coke Stevenson in the US Senate race by 87 votes. The winning margin in the disputed primary is registered in Ballot Box No. 13 in Jim Wells County.

1949 - *Aug. 24 -* The University of Texas Medical Branch in Galveston admits its first black student.

1950 - The US Supreme Court orders racial integration of The University of Texas law school.

1953 - Dwight D. Eisenhower becomes the first Texas-born President of the United States.

May 11 - A tornado kills 114, injures 597 at Waco; 150 homes and 185 other buildings are destroyed.

May 22 - The Tidelands Bill is signed by Pres. Eisenhower, giving Texas the rights to its offshore oil.

1954 - Texas women gain the right to serve on juries.

1958 - *Sept. 12 -* Integrated circuit, developed by Jack Kilby at Texas Instruments, Dallas, is successfully tested, ushering in the semiconductor and electronics age.

1961 - John Tower wins special election for US Senate, becoming the first Republican senator from Texas since Reconstruction.

1962 - NASA opens the Manned Spacecraft Center in Houston. The center moves to a new campus-like building complex in 1964. It is renamed Lyndon B. Johnson Space Center on Aug. 17, 1973.

1963 - *Nov. 22 -* President John F. Kennedy is assassinated in Dallas; vice president Lyndon B. Johnson succeeds to the office, becoming the 36th US president.

1964 - Poll tax is abolished by the 24th Amendment to the US Constitution as a requirement for voting for federal offices. It is retained in Texas, however, for state and local offices.

June 3 - San Antonio native Ed White becomes the first American to walk in space.

1966 - The poll tax is repealed as a requirement for voting in all elections by amendment of the Texas Constitution.

Barbara Jordan of Houston becomes the first black woman elected to the Texas Senate.

Aug. 1 - Charles Whitman kills 17 people, shooting them

from the observation deck of the main-building tower on The University of Texas campus in Austin.

1967 - Mexican American Legal Defense and Educational Fund (MALDEF) is incorporated in Texas; its first national office is in San Antonio.

1969 - *July 20* - Apollo 11 astronaut Neil Armstrong transmits the first words from the surface of the moon: "Houston, the Eagle has landed."

1974 - *Jan. 8* - Constitutional Convention meets to attempt to write a new state constitution. However, the delegates, comprising the membership of the 63rd Legislature, become mired in divisive politics, and the convention adjourns on July 30, 1974, without a document.

1978 - William Clements becomes the first Republican governor of Texas since Reconstruction.

1988 - Houstonian George Bush is elected president of the United States.

1990 - Democrat Ann Richards becomes the first woman governor of Texas in her own right.

1993 - *April 19* - Siege that began on Feb. 28 ended, federal agents storm the compound called Mount Carmel near Waco, where cult leader David Koresh and his followers, called Branch Davidians, had reportedly been storing a large cache of assault weapons. The assault and ensuing fire kill four agents and 86 Branch Davidians.

Republican Kay Bailey Hutchison becomes the first woman to serve as US Senator from Texas.

21st Century

2000 - Former Texas Gov. George W. Bush elected President of the United States.

- List of Texas Revolution battles -

From Wikipedia, the free encyclopedia

Battles of the Texas Revolution took place between October 2, 1835 and April 21, 1836. The Texas Revolution was fought between Mexico and rebellious colonists in Mexican Texas. All of these battles were fought within the territory of Texas.

In early 1835, Mexican president Antonio Lopez de Santa Anna began centralizing power and operating as a dictator. Federalists throughout the country revolted; in Texas, an armed uprising began on October 2 when settlers refused to return a small cannon to Mexican troops. This Battle of Gonzales ended with Mexican troops retreating to San Antonio de Bexar (modern-day San Antonio, Texas) empty-handed. Emboldened by their victory, the Texians formed a volunteer army. A small force of Texians travelled down the Texas coastline, defeating Mexican troops at Goliad and at Fort Lipantitlán. The majority of Texian troops followed General Stephen F. Austin to Bexar, where they initiated a siege of the Mexican garrison. After victories in several skirmishes, including the Battle of Concepción and the Grass Fight, Texians attacked Bexar. After several days of fighting, the Siege of Bexar ended with the surrender of Mexican general Martin Perfecto de Cos. With the parole of Cos's troops back to Mexico in mid-December, no Mexican forces remained in Texas.

Many Texians believed the war was now over, and the majority of the settlers returned to their homes. The remaining troops were garrisoned at the Alamo Mission in Bexar and at Presidio La Bahia in Goliad. In early January, a large number of the remaining soldiers, most of them adventurers recently arrived from the United States, began clamoring to invade Mexico. Colonel Frank W. Johnson and Dr. James Grant began preparing to attack Matamoros.

Even before Cos's defeat, Santa Anna had been making plans to retake Texas. In January, he led the Army of Operations in Texas towards the rebellious territory. At the Rio Grande, the army separated; Santa Anna led the bulk of the troops toward Bexar, where he laid siege to the Alamo. The remaining troops, under General Jose de Urrea, travelled up the coastline, quickly defeating Johnson and Grant at the battles of San Patricio and Agua Dulce. News of these first Mexican victories cheered the Mexican force gathered at Bexar. On March 6, Santa Anna ordered an assault on the Alamo; all but a few of the defenders were killed. News of the Texian defeat and march of the Mexican army terrified the settlers; in an event later known as the Runaway Scrape, settlers, the Texas government, and the remnants of the Texian army under the command of Sam Houston fled east, away from the oncoming army. Houston ordered Colonel James Fannin to abandon Goliad and join his retreat. Fannin delayed his departure and sent a small number of troops to help the settlers at Refugio to evacuate. Urrea's men surprised the Texians at Refugio and quickly defeated them. After receiving word of the defeat, Fannin finally began his retreat, but his men were quickly overtaken by Mexican soldiers. Fannin surrendered after the Battle of Coleto. He and his 300 men were taken prisoner and days later executed in the Goliad Massacre.

The only remaining Texian troops were those retreating with Houston. After learning that Santa Anna had again divided his forces, Houston ordered an attack on April 21, 1836. Crying "Remember the Alamo" and "Remember Goliad", the Texians showed little mercy during the Battle of San Jacinto. Santa Anna was captured the following day and ordered his army to return to Mexico, ending the Texas Revolution.

Key
(M) – Mexican victory
(T) – Texian victory

Battle	Location	Date(s)	Engagement remarks	Victor
Battle of Gonzales	Gonzales	October 2, 1835	This battle resulted in the first casualties of the Texas Revolution. One Texian soldier was injured, and one Mexican soldier was killed.	T

Battle	Location	Date(s)	Engagement remarks	Victor
Battle of Goliad	Goliad	October 10, 1835	Texians captured Presidio La Bahia, blocking the Mexican Army in Texas from accessing the primary Texas port of Copano. One Texian was wounded, and estimates of Mexican casualties range from one to three soldiers killed and from three to seven wounded.	T
Battle of Lipantitlán	San Patricio	November 4-5, 1835	Texians captured and destroyed Fort Lipantitlán. Most of the Mexican soldiers retreated to Matamoros. One Texian was wounded, and 3-5 Mexican soldiers were killed, with an additional 14-17 Mexican soldiers wounded.	T
Battle of Concepción	San Antonio de Bexar	October 28, 1835	In the last offensive ordered by General Martin Perfecto de Cos during the Texas Revolution, Mexican soldiers surprised a Texian force camped near Mission Concepción. The Texians repulsed several attacks with what historian Alwyn Barr described as "able leadership, a strong position, and greater firepower". One Texian was injured, and Richard Andrews became the first Texian soldier to die in battle. Between 14 and 76 Mexican soldiers were killed. Historian Stephen Hardin believes that "the relative ease of the victory at Concepción instilled in the Texians a reliance on their long rifles and a contempt for their enemies", which may have led to the later Texian defeat at Coleto.	T
Grass Fight	San Antonio de Bexar	November 26, 1835	4 Texians wounded and 17 Mexican casualties.	T
Siege of Bexar	San Antonio de Bexar	October 12-December 11, 1835	After a six-week siege, Texians attacked Bexar and fought from house to house for five days. After Cos surrendered, all Mexican troops in Texas were forced to retreat beyond the Rio Grande, leaving the Texians in military control.	T

Battle	Location	Date(s)	Engagement remarks	Victor
Battle of San Patricio	San Patricio	February 27, 1836	This was the first battle of the Goliad Campaign, and the first battle of the Texas Revolution in which the Mexican Army was the victor. Part of Johnson-Grant Forces-who were also defeated at Battle of Agua Dulce.	M
Battle of Agua Dulce		March 2, 1836	Second battle of the Goliad Campaign. Of 27 men of Johnson-Grant forces-12/15 killed; 6 captured; Six escaped, of whom five were killed at Goliad Massacre.	M
Battle of the Alamo	San Antonio de Bexar	February 23-March 6, 1836	Mexican President Antonio Lopez de Santa Anna personally oversaw the siege of the Alamo and the subsequent battle, where almost all Texian defenders were killed. Anger over Santa Anna's lack of mercy led many Texian settlers to join the Texian Army.	M
Battle of Refugio	Refugio	March 14, 1836	Third battle of the Goliad Campaign.	M
Battle of Coleto	outside Goliad	March 19-20, 1836	Final battle of the Goliad Campaign. Approximately 300 of the captured Texians were executed on March 27 in the Goliad Massacre.	M
Battle of San Jacinto		April 21, 1836	After an 18-minute battle, Texians routed Santa Anna's forces, eventually taking Santa Anna prisoner. This was the last battle of the Texas Revolution.	T

About the Authors

Manuel L. (Manny) English, Ph.D.
Visit Manny's website at: www.drmannyenglish.com

Dr. Manuel (Manny) L. English is a retired executive and former professor. He was born in East Texas, one of ten children of sharecropper parents. When he was five years old, he began working in the cotton and corn fields along with his brothers and sisters attending school only when there was no work. Poverty prevailed in all directions. From the age of ten there·were many moves to Arkansas and several parts of Texas in search of farm work.

At sixteen, to escape the poverty of his childhood, Manny enlisted in the U.S. Marines Corps serving in Korea with the 1st Marine Division. Two weeks after returning to Camp Pendleton, he came down with Korean malaria spending 40 days in a military hospital. This near-death experience gave him the opportunity to realize that he wanted to make something out of his life. He left active duty in the fall of 1955.

After some travel and not quite ready to settle down, he joined the U.S. Army in 1957 spending six years serving in Berlin, Germany and at Schofield Barracks, Hawaii. Manny met Jeanette in Honolulu in February 1962 and they married six months later.

In 1964, he elected to leave the army and attend university. Two months later, a U.S. Air Force recruiter came and asked him to join. With one child and one on the way, and with the promise of support in getting his university degree, he enlisted as a staff sergeant in the

Air Force. Ten months later Manny was selected for the 'Boot Strap' program spending a full calendar year at the University of Omaha earning his bachelor's degree. He was then immediately promoted to second lieutenant. The Air Force continued its educational support enabling Manny to earn masters (U of Oklahoma) and doctorate (U of Manchester, England) degrees. Manny retired from the U.S. Air Force in 1976. He is proud to hold the title: Marine, Soldier, and Airman.

Manny went on to teach at several universities and serve as chief executive officer of a number of medical organizations including two teaching hospitals, one in Saudi Arabia. He has published numerous articles on a variety of subject and his book titled: An Imaginative Existence - A Provocative Essay on Causation, Manifestation, and Finality of Being is a Pinnacle Award Winner for 2010 . He now resides in the Seattle area and his interests include fictional and non-fictional writing.

Chris Adams, Major General, USAF (Ret)
Visit Chris's website at: www.literarywerks.com

Chris Adams grew up in the small town of Tomball, Texas. He is a retired U.S. Air Force Major General, former Chief of Staff, Strategic Air Command; Associate Director, Los Alamos National Laboratory, industry executive and published author. As a basis for several of his works, he traveled extensively in the former Soviet States, making some 23 extended visits. He draws extensively on his knowledge and experience in strategic air operations, nuclear weapons and the culture of the former Soviet Union in developing his writings.

A veteran of Vietnam, he served as a bomber pilot, wing and air division commander and senior staff officer, three years with the Joint Chiefs of Staff and six years with the Defense Nuclear Agency. He is a Texan and American Patriot, and has been awarded the nation's highest peacetime decoration, The United States Distinguished Service Medal, The Daughters of the American

Revolution (DAR) National Medal of Honor and numerous other awards and decorations. He is a Distinguished Alumnus of Tarleton State University, Texas A&M University-Commerce and is listed in Who's Who in America. His previous books include three non-fiction Cold War historical treatments and four spy novels.

Books by Chris Adams

Non-fiction
Inside The Cold War: A Cold Warrior's Reflections, 1999
Ideologies in Conflict: A Cold War Docu-Story, 2001
Deterrence: An Enduring Strategy, 2009

Fiction
Red Eagle: A Cold War Espionage Story, 2000
Profiles in Betrayal: The Enemy Within, 2002
The Betrayal Mosaic: A Cold War Spy Story, 2004
Out of Darkness: The Last Russian Revolution, 2006
Requiem of a Spy, 2010